Katy's Exmoor Friends

The Final Part of the Trilogy

By Victoria Eveleigh

Illustrated by Chris Eveleigh

Tortoise
Publishing

We would like to thank everyone who helped
and encouraged us in the production of this book.
Particular thanks to Sally Chapman-Walker for designing
the book, and Marcia Monbleau, Sue and Emily Croft, Sue Baker,
Ann Mold and Laura Garner for their help and advice.

Photographs
Inside front cover by Nick Eveleigh.
Inside back cover by Betty Perks.

In writing this story, every attempt has been made to make it
true to Exmoor by using local names, while avoiding the use of
specific names of people and farms known to the author.
The characters in this story are fictitious, and any resemblance to
real people is purely coincidental.

Printed in great Britain by Toptown Printers Limited
w.w.w.toptown.co.uk

Book Design by Sally Chapman-Walker

Published and distributed by
Tortoise Publishing,
West Ilkerton Farm,
Lynton, Exmoor,
North Devon EX35 6QA
Tel/Fax (01598) 752310
Email info@tortoise-publishing.co.uk
Website www.tortoise-publishing.co.uk

This book is dedicated to
Tinkerbell

Katy's Exmoor Friends

Contents

"It is scarce possible, in the animal world, to behold anything prettier than a drove of Exmoor Ponies."

F. J. Snell *A Book of Exmoor* 1903

Chapter 1
New Neighbours

As Katy rode her Exmoor pony, Trifle, along the lane from Barton Farm, she felt she was the luckiest girl in the world. The whole summer holidays lay ahead, like a bulging Christmas stocking waiting to be explored: most of the contents half-expected, but some complete surprises tucked in between. Katy knew there would be horse shows, Pony Club camp, picnics, the beach, long rides, lazy days and having fun with her best friend, Alice. But the surprises — well, if she knew what they were going to be, they wouldn't be surprises.

"Next week it's Pony Club camp, Trifle. I'm afraid you'll have to go because poor old Jacko's still lame from that horrid nail he trod on last winter. Anyway, now that you're four, it will do you good to have a bit of proper schooling. You'll learn how to jump, too; that'll be fun!" Katy leant forward and pretended to ride like a jockey. Trifle felt the shift in her weight and started to trot, and then canter. Laughing at the eagerness of her pony, Katy sat up straight again, and Trifle eased back into a steady trot.

They rounded a sharp bend, and Trifle skidded to a halt. Katy bumped her nose on Trifle's neck, and just managed to save herself from falling off by grabbing a handful of bushy mane.

The lane was blocked by a huge removal lorry. A couple of men in blue overalls were using a very noisy electric ramp to unload furniture, supervised by a dark-haired man wearing a black leather jacket and blue jeans.

"Crikey!" Katy exclaimed. "Wellsworthy Farm must have been sold! That was quick! We can't get past the lorry, so I suppose we'll have to turn back."

"Hi, there!" the man in the leather jacket shouted, raising his hand in greeting. "Hang on a minute!"

Katy tried her best to hang on a minute; Trifle was dancing on the spot with agitation. The man's eyes were hidden by expensive-looking sunglasses but, as he came closer, Katy could see a smile on his lined, suntanned face. He gave Trifle a hearty pat on the neck, which was more like hitting than patting, and she tried to shy away.

"Nice little Shetland pony you've got there," the man said, nimbly avoiding Trifle's hooves as they tap-danced on the tarmac. He talked like someone on Eastenders. "We've just bought this place. Who are you? I'm Dean, by the way."

Katy was just about to speak when Dean gave Trifle another slap and asked, "What's his name?" Trifle spun round, pushing Dean to one side.

"Oops! Sorry!" Katy said. "I'm Katy Squires, and I live at Barton Farm, about a mile up that lane. This is my Exmoor pony, Trifle. She's a mare — a girl, not a boy."

"Exmoor, Shetland, mare, stallion — they're all

the same to me, darling. Dangerous at both ends and uncomfortable in the middle. Hang about! You're the girl who was on the telly with a pony who saved somebody's life! Is that the pony?" Dean gave Trifle another hit-pat, and she decided she'd had enough.

"Yes, she is. Sorry! Got to go! Nice to meet you!" Katy said quickly, as Trifle set off down the lane, galloping sideways.

"I like the circus trick!" Dean called out. "What do you do for an encore?"

Katy barely heard him above the noise of Trifle's clattering hooves as she flew round the corner, heading for the safety of home.

Katy's mother, Sally, was in the brand-new kitchen at Barton Farm. She was talking on the telephone to Melanie, who was Alice's mother. Through their daughters' friendship, Sally and Melanie had become close friends. Sally often treated herself to long telephone conversations when her family were out of the house. Housework could be a lonely job.

"Yes, the kitchen's wonderful! I'm afraid to cook anything in case I make a mess. To tell the truth, a lot of things have changed since the spring. Our money worries are over, thank goodness, but now that Phil is running these residential painting courses full-time we hardly see each other. I'm stuck here in the house, cooking and cleaning all the time, and he's out in the studio with the guests. Tom's in charge of the farm now, of course, and that's causing a bit of friction. Although he learnt all the theory at college, he's still got a lot to learn and he won't accept help or advice from anyone — not even his Granfer. It's such a pity Greg has gone to Australia. He was a good friend to Tom, and a great help on the farm." Sally lowered her voice to a loud whisper. "Between you and me, I think Katy is a bit taken with Greg, even though she's thirteen and he's twenty two. A school girl's crush, really. He sends her e-mails from Australia, which is sweet of him.... Oh! Katy's just come in. Take your boots off before you come into the kitchen, please, young lady!"

"Oops! Sorry, Mum. I just need a bucket of warm water from the sink so I can wash Trifle. She's a bit hot and sweaty because..."

"Oh, go on then, but don't spill any. I'm talking to Melanie."

"Ask her if it's still OK to go round to Stonyford this afternoon. Alice and I want to get everything sorted for camp."

"Melanie heard you, and she says that's fine. She'll give you a lesson on Trifle, too, if you hurry."

"Cool! Thanks!" Katy said and rushed off, sloshing water onto the floor from her swinging bucket.

Sally sighed. "Sorry, Melanie, where were we? Oh yes, I know what I wanted to tell you. Apparently, Wellsworthy Farm has been sold, and the new people are moving in this week. Nancy in the Post Office said they're from London. The man is very rich — he made his money dealing in celebrities' cars. His girlfriend looks like a Barbie doll: blonde hair, sun tan and slim legs which seem to end at her armpits. I don't expect they'll stay here long. One wet winter, and they'll be running back to London."

At that moment, Tom, Katy's 21 year-old brother, walked into the kitchen, his boots plastered with cow dung. He put a slimy lump of metal, covered with very smelly dung, onto the scrubbed pine table.

"Ugh! Tom, how could you?" Sally said. "Get that filthy thing out of here! Look at the mess your boots are making!" She turned back to the telephone and said, "Sorry, I'd better go."

"Well, you don't expect me to wear socks with

all this water on the floor, do you?" Tom asked. "I need to telephone Mole Valley Farmers and order a new bearing for the muck spreader." He took a clean dishcloth and started to rub some dung off the lump of metal on the table, searching for a part number.

"Tom, for goodness sake..."

"Keep your hair on, mother. I'll clear it up in a minute. You've got to expect a bit of muck in a farmhouse kitchen," Tom said, patting her newly washed hair affectionately with his grubby hand.

After his phone call, Tom went outside, leaving Sally to clear away all the mess in her not-so-brand-new kitchen. Running exclusive residential art courses and a farm from the same house was not going to be easy.

Katy rode to Stonyford by the field and moorland route, avoiding the Wellsworthy lane. There were several gates on the way up to the moor, which meant she could practise one of the tricks she was teaching Trifle — pushing gates open. Katy would undo the latch and then say, "Push, Trifle," and the pony would push the gate open by leaning against it.

The journey seemed to take longer than usual, probably because Katy couldn't wait to see Alice again. They had remained best friends even though they now went to different schools; Katy went to the local secondary school, Ilfracombe College, and Alice went to a boarding school miles away. This made the holidays even more special for the two friends, and they spent as much time as possible with each other.

Melanie owned Stonyford Riding Stables, which was gaining the reputation of being the best riding school on Exmoor. Katy loved going there, and she knew Trifle did, too. The pony arched her neck and showed off by pointing her toes as they cantered over the close-cropped moorland heather, and she whinnied a greeting to announce their arrival. When Trifle whinnied, her whole body shook. It was like sitting on a mini-earthquake, and Katy couldn't help giggling.

"Behold! Trifle the Wonder Horse!" Alice announced with extreme grandness as she opened the gate and bowed with a flourish. "Are you too famous to grace our humble home now that you're a TV celebrity? We'll have to feed you chocolate-coated apples, and put champagne in your water buckets, while you recline on a goose feather bed."

"If you're not careful, she'll stay here for

ever," Katy laughed.

"Why, hello!" said Alice in mock surprise. "I didn't see you up there! How are you, Katy? Long time no see!"

"Oh, it's so great to see you again, Alice!" Katy said. Then she made a clicking sound with her tongue and Trifle instantly dropped her head to the ground so Katy could slide down her neck. "Tra-lah! That's our latest trick."

"Trifle! Is there no end to your talents?" Alice asked.

That question was answered the following week at Pony Club camp.

CHAPTER 2
Pony Club Camp

Pony Club camp was one of the highlights of Katy's year, as it was for many members. It was a matter of pride to have all the right kit for camp — new water buckets, hay nets, brushes, jodhpurs and countless other "essentials" — so the tack shop owners of Exmoor thought it was a highlight of the year, too.

The first evening of camp was great fun. There was a general air of excitement and anticipation, with several good-natured hay fights and water fights. Everyone wanted to meet Trifle because they had seen all the television reports and newspaper articles about her medal for the daring rescue earlier in the year. A tame Exmoor pony is a bit of a novelty — even on Exmoor — so a tame and famous Exmoor pony was irresistible.

"She's so sweet!" said Fiona.

"Adorable!" agreed Susan.

"And so huggable!" said Sophie.

"You're so lucky, Katy!" said Claire.

If Katy were a cat, she would have purred.

Katy and Alice had persuaded Melanie to let them sleep in her four-berth caravan during camp. The caravan was like a palace compared to the small, damp tent they had shared in previous years.

As it turned out, camp was a washout for Katy, and not just because it rained. In other years, she had been with Jacko, her 13.2 hands high Welsh Cob cross Thoroughbred gelding. Tragically, he had stepped on the upturned nail of a cast shoe the previous winter, and he was still lame. Jacko was the sort of pony that horsy people call "a push-button pony." Riding him, Katy had progressed quickly from a beginner to a competent rider, and they had won many trophies and rosettes to prove the success of their partnership. Jacko made riding easy. Katy had even allowed herself to feel slightly superior when she saw other people having problems, like their ponies bucking or refusing to jump.

A favourite saying amongst horsy people is, "Pride comes before a fall."

At the beginning of camp, Katy was in the third ride with several friends of a similar age. They had a very good-looking teacher called Tony, who was a volunteer instructor from the King's Troop Royal Horse Artillery. Trifle was the smallest pony in the group; in fact, most of the other children had horses. It soon became obvious that Trifle had been put in the wrong class. When the ride was walking, Trifle had to jog to keep up, and when they were trotting, she cantered. All the horses in the class were good at jumping, but Trifle would not even walk over a brightly painted trotting pole; she behaved as if it were a poisonous snake. Tony suggested tactfully that both Trifle and Katy would be happier in a less demanding ride with smaller ponies. Katy did not want to leave her friends, but she knew Tony was right. She was transferred to the lowest ride, with smaller ponies and younger — much younger — children.

Val, the teacher of the lowest ride, was new to the area. She had telephoned Mrs. Edwards, the Pony Club District Commissioner, a couple of weeks before camp to offer her services as an instructor. Val was very selective in what she told Mrs. Edwards. She told her that she was 42 years old, a fully qualified riding instructor, and had moved from Wiltshire where she had taught in a riding school. Mrs. Edwards also heard the life histories of Val's two prize-winning Connemara ponies. However, Val did not tell her that she had been sacked from three teaching jobs because of her quick temper and objectionable behaviour.

Mrs. Edwards did not usually take on new instructors for camp without trying them out at a few rallies beforehand, but she was desperately in need of someone to teach the younger children and Val seemed to have all the right qualifications.

"Would you mind taking the younger ones?" Mrs. Edwards asked hopefully. "They're not very good at jumping, so they always perform a musical ride for the parents on the final day. Of course, you can do some jumping during the week, but the main thing is to work towards the musical ride. Would that be possible?"

At its best, a musical ride is like an elegant formation dance on horseback in time to music. With spirited children and naughty ponies, a musical ride is not always at its best.

"No problem!" Val said enthusiastically. "As a matter of fact, musical rides are one of my specialities — I love to create order out of chaos."

Mrs. Edwards thought Val was trying to be funny, so she laughed. "Well, that's marvellous! Absolutely marvellous!" she said.

Val was not a good riding teacher. She liked instant results and perfection, and yet she had chosen a career working with ponies and children. It had turned her into a bad-tempered bully. If children didn't do as they were told, she shouted at them and insulted them. If ponies didn't do as they were told, she resorted to almost anything to "win" whatever battle she had started. The arrival of Katy and Trifle after lunch on the first day of camp annoyed Val intensely. They turned her nice, even ride of eight into an uneven ride of nine; her plans for a delightfully symmetrical musical ride were ruined.

The first two days of camp were spent practising for the musical ride, but without the music.

A sound system was going to be hired, at great expense, so the children could perform to music in front of their parents. In the meantime, everyone had to make do with Val shouting, "Pom! Pom! Pom! Pom!" in time to an imaginary tune. This wasn't anyone's idea of fun, least of all Trifle's. Although Katy had done a bit of schooling with Trifle at Stonyford, it had always been in short, carefully structured lessons under Melanie's supervision. Most of Trifle's experience of being ridden had, until camp, involved going out for enjoyable rides. Going round in circles for hours with Val shouting all the time was not enjoyable. Trifle gradually turned from a sweet-natured, eager pony into a bored, tired kick-along pony.

On Tuesday evening there was a spectacular thunderstorm and it poured with rain. Sophie and Claire's tent was flooded so, giggling and dripping, they joined Alice and Katy in the caravan.

Listening to the other three girls laughing and talking enthusiastically about what a fantastic time they were having made Katy feel isolated and miserable. Alice was in the top ride, but Sophie and Claire were in Tony's ride — the one

Katy had been in at first. It appeared that all the girls loved Tony and he was a brilliant, fun teacher. Katy decided to ask Val if they could do some jumping the following day, for Trifle's sake as much as hers, before they both died of boredom.

The next morning, Katy gathered the children in her group together before Val arrived for the morning lesson. "I'm sick of doing this musical ride, aren't you?" she asked. "Shall we ask if we can do some jumping today for a change?"

"Yeah, wicked!" said one boy.

"Good-eee! Merrylegs loves jumping," said a very small girl on a very small grey pony.

"Hurray! Mutiny!" yelled Tim, standing up in his stirrups and waving his whip in the air. "Oh, Val! Hello. Katy was just telling us her good idea."

Surprisingly, Val did not tell Tim off for standing up in his stirrups and waving his whip in the air. Instead, she walked up to Katy and said sarcastically, "It's a pity that good ideas don't go with good riding, isn't it? Then you wouldn't be in the bottom group with people half your size."

Some of the boys sniggered.

Val's comments were so unexpected, hurtful

16

and unjust that Katy felt as if she'd been punched in the stomach. She was acutely aware that she was the largest in her ride. She looked down at Trifle's mane, and it blurred as tears pricked at her eyes. "Trifle is only four years old, and she hasn't done much work — riding on the moor, mainly," she mumbled.

"Hmm. I must admit your parents do seem to have been very foolish in buying you an Exmoor pony, of all things. And a young Exmoor, at that," Val said.

"But they didn't!" Katy explained. "I bought her with my own money from Brendon Pony Sale, when she was a foal."

"Well then, you have only yourself to blame, haven't you?" Val said triumphantly, and she swaggered off to her position of command in front of the class. "This morning we shall do some jumping," she announced.

Val had planned to do jumping anyway.

To begin with, the lesson went remarkably well — when they weren't actually jumping. Their first exercise was to trot over trotting poles in jumping position. The top classes had all the coloured show jump poles, so Katy's class had only rustic poles. Trifle didn't mind trotting over rustic poles; they were like fallen branches. She didn't even mind when the last pole was raised slightly so she had to lift her legs high to trot over it, as she did when trotting through deep heather. However, once the pole became too high to trot over, she stopped in front of it and tried to go round the side. To Trifle, it probably seemed a very sensible thing to do, but Val was not impressed. Katy was told to try the jump again, and Val ran behind, shouting and waving her whip.

Trifle skidded to a halt in front of the jump and then, faced with a shouting madwoman behind her, did an enormous cat-leap over the jump. Katy was taken by surprise. She shrieked, gripped the reins to steady herself, accidentally jabbed Trifle in the mouth and bit her own tongue. Trifle stopped immediately after the jump; the horrible pain in her mouth when she was mid-air had told her that Katy wanted to stop as soon as possible. Katy fell off Trifle for the first time in her life.

Suddenly, Trifle was really frightened. Nobody had ever fallen from her before, and it was one bad experience too many. She bolted to the far end of the field, next to where Claire and Sophie were having a lesson with Tony.

"Oh, look!" cried Claire. "There's Trifle! Katy must have fallen off."

Tony caught Trifle and led her back to Val's ride. Katy was sitting on the ground, gasping for air, and Val seemed to be ignoring her.

"Are you OK, Katy?" Tony asked kindly.

"She's fine thank you, Anthony. Just a bit winded, that's all. Don't worry; the pony won't get away with this."

"Are you OK, Katy?" Tony repeated anxiously.

"Y-yes, I th-think so," Katy gasped. She wished she had more breath so she could tell Tony what had happened.

"Thank you, Anthony," Val said coldly. "I can deal with this, now. You really shouldn't leave your ride unattended."

Tony walked back to his ride. He had heard Val shouting at her class for the past three days, and he was worried. In his opinion, she shouldn't have been put in charge of a hamster, let alone nine young children and their ponies. As he got back to his ride, he looked over his shoulder and saw that Val had mounted Trifle and was lengthening her stirrups. "Sophie and Claire," Tony said. "Would you ride up to the top field and fetch Mrs. Edwards? Ask her to come straight away, please."

Sophie and Claire were only too willing to oblige, and they cantered off to find the District Commissioner.

Trifle was nervous. There was an unfamiliar, rough person on her back. The pony had known only kindness and love from Katy, but she could feel the anger of her present rider like electric shocks running through her whole body.

Katy could hardly bear to watch her pony looking so unhappy and frightened. It went against all Katy's upbringing to question an adult, but she knew that what Val was doing was wrong — very wrong. "Please be gentle with her! She didn't mean to be naughty! She's never jumped before," Katy pleaded tearfully as Val rode Trifle around the arena in trot, and then canter, before heading for the jump.

Trifle refused the jump, and Val whipped her. It was the first time in her life she'd been whipped, and it terrified her. She leapt over the jump from a standstill, and Val accidentally jabbed her in the mouth, so she stopped after the jump and was whipped again. This made her buck out of shear desperation, and she was whipped again.

"Don't! Please don't! You're hurting her! She doesn't understand!" Katy shouted. She couldn't believe what was happening. Her kind, beautiful, intelligent, trusting and fun-loving pony was being hurt, and Katy felt powerless to stop it. How could Val be so vicious and stupid?

"She can't get away with this, Katy! She's got to learn who's boss. It may seem harsh, but I know what I'm doing," Val said rather breathlessly as she turned for the jump a second time and urged Trifle into a canter by making what she thought was an encouraging clicking noise with her tongue. Even in her fright and bewilderment, Trifle recognized the sound of clicking as the command to let her rider dismount by sliding down her neck. Quick as a flash, she skidded to a halt and put her head down, and her rider dismounted by sliding down her neck.

Mrs Edwards saw everything as she hurried down the hill. Val was taken to hospital, but she had no serious injuries — except to her pride. She never taught the Pony Club again.

It was decided that for the remaining two days of camp the second and third rides would be combined, leaving Tony free to teach Katy's ride.

All the parents agreed that the musical ride was the most entertaining show they'd ever seen. This was probably because it wasn't strictly a musical ride — it was more like a series of circus acts set to the song Crazy Horses, and it stretched the Pony Club health and safety rules to the limit. Merrylegs, ridden bareback, jumped a line of small jumps, Tim gave a vaulting display, and each child was given the chance to do something he, or she, was good at. As the smiling, breathless riders lined up to take a bow after the grand finale, Katy and Trifle — who were symmetrically placed in the centre of the line, with four ponies on either side — walked forward a few paces. Katy clicked her tongue and Trifle lowered her head to the ground, as if she were taking a bow, to delighted applause from the audience. Katy wasn't allowed to dismount by sliding down Trifle's neck; Pony Club rules forbid that sort of thing because it can be dangerous.

CHAPTER 3
Competition Mix

Katy was so tired after getting home from camp that she slept until lunchtime the next day. When she went downstairs, her grandfather and her Aunt Rachel were sitting at the kitchen table, while Sally made lunch. Katy adored Granfer and Rachel, and there were hugs and kisses all round.

"Pull up a chair and tell us about camp. I hear you had a teacher from hell, but good old Trifle got the better of her!" Granfer said. "As the old joke goes, the pony stopped with a jerk and the jerk fell off!"

Katy couldn't help laughing, although she felt upset every time she thought about Val riding Trifle. "Yes, that's just what happened," she said. "Oh, Granfer! Val was so horrible! I'm terribly worried that Trifle's been put off jumping for good."

"Don't you worry, Katy. I expect her confidence has taken a bit of a battering, but Rachel will soon sort her out for you," Granfer replied. "It will help take her mind off Moon."

Katy looked at Rachel properly for the first time. She appeared to have been crying. "Oh, Rachel! What's happened to Moon?"

"Don't worry, nothing's seriously the matter. I mean, he won't have to be put down or anything," Rachel said. "He's had a dry cough, on and off, and he sometimes gets unusually short of breath, so I decided to get the vet to check him over. She's found Moon has mild COPD. Although it can be kept in check with medicine and good management, his lungs are damaged and he won't stand the strain of being a top-class eventer."

Katy was puzzled. "What on earth is COPD?"

"Well, its proper name is chronic obstructive pulmonary disease. It's a bit like asthma and it's triggered by dust and fungus in mouldy hay or bedding, which sets off an allergic reaction. I haven't a clue what started it. I'm always so fussy about the bedding and feed at the stables."

"I bet it started in that horrible dealer's yard where we rescued him last year!" Katy said. "I remember thinking that the stables smelt odd — sort of damp and musty. Come to think of it, he had a cough and a runny nose when we took him back to Stonyford, but I thought it was a cold."

"Oh dear, I never should have sold him!" Rachel said, and she began to cry. "It's all my fault!"

"Rubbish! No way is it your fault! It's just rotten bad luck. Please stop crying, Rachel!" Katy said, putting an arm round her aunt's shaking shoulders.

Between diminishing sobs, Rachel said, "Oh dear, I feel so guilty about it all, and I'm so disappointed. I was certain that somehow Moon and I would make it all the way to Badminton. I know Mr. Jackson owns him now, but I still think of Moon as my horse of a lifetime. He's just so special. Mr. Jackson will be really disappointed, too. I haven't told him yet."

"I'm sure he'll understand, Rachel. He's so nice and kind. It's just bad luck — I'm certain he won't blame you," Katy reassured her.

"I expect he'll say what I said," Granfer said dryly.

"What was that, Granfer?"

"That's horses for you!"

After lunch, Katy and Rachel went to see Trifle. If anyone could help Trifle conquer her fear of jumping, it would be Rachel; she had a special way of communicating with horses, and Trifle adored her.

"Well, she's still friendly!" Rachel commented as Trifle trotted over to the gate and nuzzled Rachel affectionately. "But she's looking very slim, isn't she? Trifle, the supermodel!"

Katy giggled. "I expect it was all that trotting in silly circles with vile Val. It knocked all the fun out of her, Rachel. It worries me, because I've entered her for Exford and Dunster shows, and they're on Wednesday the fourteenth of August and Friday the sixteenth — in less than two weeks! It would be so embarrassing if she looked grumpy and fell asleep in front of the judges."

"You haven't entered her for any jumping classes, have you?"

"No, thank goodness."

"Good. Then our first mission is to get Trifle enjoying life again. Lots of fun rides with Alice, and small — and I mean small — amounts of nuts or coarse mix fed morning and evening should pep her up a bit. I'm pretty busy getting ready for the shows, too; we're taking six horses to Exford and four to Dunster. Afterwards, I should have a bit more time to help you re-train Trifle to jump. I'll come over next weekend, and we'll go through your ridden and in-hand shows, if you like."

Katy hugged her aunt. "Oh, yes please! I need all the help I can get. Thanks, Rachel!"

That evening, Rachel went to Mr. Jackson's house near Winsford. He owned Moon, and he was financing Rachel's attempt to qualify for Badminton, so she wanted to tell him the sad news herself.

As usual, he was incredibly kind and understanding. "That's horses for you," he said. "It sounds as if Moon will be fine for normal work, as long as we're careful, and I expect he would far rather have a life of hacking and hunting than all that high pressure training, travelling and eventing. Perhaps it's all for the best, you know." He poured himself a gin and tonic. "Are you sure you won't have a drink, Rachel?"

"No thanks, Mr. Jackson. I've gone off alcohol,

and coffee and tea. A glass of water would be lovely, though."

"Not pregnant, are you?" Mr. Jackson asked, half joking.

"Um, I'm beginning to think I might be," said Rachel.

"Well, good for you, my dear girl!" Mr. Jackson said. "I bet Mark is delighted, isn't he?"

"To tell the truth I haven't told anyone yet; I have to be sure, first. Mark has wanted a family ever since we got married, so I know he'll be thrilled. I must admit that I'm really excited, too, although I don't know what I'll do about my job at Exford Stables. Please keep this a secret for a few weeks, Mr. Jackson, until I'm certain."

"Don't worry, my dear girl. I won't tell a soul. It's funny how things have a mysterious way of turning out for the best in the end, isn't it?" Mr. Jackson said, smiling with genuine pleasure.

Not for the first time, Rachel was bowled over by Mr. Jackson's kindness.

The following day, Tom had to go to Mole Valley Farmers in South Molton to pick up the spare part for his muck spreader which had, at last, been delivered. Katy went with him so she could buy some feed for Trifle. She decided to buy coarse mix, because it looked more appetising than pony nuts.

"Three bags of coarse mix, please," Katy said to the man at the counter.

"Which do you want? We've got Alfalfa Added Mix, Calming and Conditioning Mix, Competition Mix, Herbal Health Mix, Standard Mix, Stud Mix, Sustained Energy Mix, Ultra Light Slimming Mix or Veteran Mix."

Katy felt flustered; she had no idea there were so many different types of coarse mix. Trifle was being prepared for two important shows, so Competition Mix sounded good. "Competition Mix, please," Katy said confidently.

Trifle clearly approved of Katy's choice. She munched through the generous portion in her bucket in next to no time, so Katy gave her a smaller second helping. She also gave Jacko some food so he didn't feel left out.

By the weekend, Trifle was beside herself with pent-up energy, and she was jumpy and bad-tempered. Alarmingly, she had also started to buck and shy, and she pulled terribly when trotting or cantering. If she were a human, she would have changed from a hard-working, law-abiding citizen into a lager lout on the rampage. Katy was really worried, and thought it must be due to delayed stress from camp. One thing was certain: Trifle couldn't go to any shows in her present state of mind.

Luckily, Rachel arrived on Saturday afternoon. She listened to Katy's woeful tales of Trifle's bad behaviour, saw how much Competition Mix Trifle had eaten in the past few days and — to Katy's dismay — burst out laughing.

"Oh, Katy! You are a silly ninny! Competition Mix is a high energy mix for large horses like Moon when they're doing a lot of work. Small native ponies like Trifle just don't need that sort of food. No wonder she's gone a bit loopy!"

Katy looked crestfallen. "But you said…"

"Yes, I know I told you to feed a few nuts or a bit of coarse mix. It's my fault — I should have explained about the different types and the amount you should feed. Don't worry, I doubt if there's any harm done, but it's lucky I came over before she went completely bananas or got laminitis from too much food. We'd better put her to work and get rid of some of that excess energy, eh?"

After Katy's lesson, Rachel said, "There's no possibility of her falling asleep in front of the judges, anyway!"

By Tuesday — the day before Exford Show —

Trifle had, thankfully, calmed down a lot. Katy was getting a lift to the show with Melanie and Alice, so she rode over to Stonyford on Tuesday afternoon. Preparing for a show with a friend made all the hard work fun, especially when the friend was Alice. The girls were so excited they hardly slept at all that night.

CHAPTER 4
Showtime

Exford Show is organised by the Devon and Somerset Staghounds, and the Exmoor Pony Society has its annual breed show at the far end of the showground on the same day. People travel with their Exmoor ponies from all over Britain to take part.

As Katy drove through the gates to the showground of the 109th Exford Horse Show, she hoped Trifle would behave better than she had as a two year-old. Then, both Katy and Trifle had been very inexperienced. Now, they were older and wiser, but Trifle had been very excited that morning — neighing, tossing her head and barging into everyone. This was the only year they could take part in the junior classes, where riders had to be under 14 years old and their ponies had to be four or over. Granfer would be watching, and Katy was very anxious that he should be proud of them.

Trifle charged down the ramp of the Stonyford lorry as if she were being chased by demons, and her coat was sticky with sweat. Her first class of the day — for in-hand mares over four years and under nine years — was called immediately to the collecting ring, so Katy had no time to groom Trifle and calm her down. There were 15 ponies in the class, and Trifle was the worst behaved by far. Katy could barely hold her as she charged round the ring, anxiously whinnying for her travelling companions. They were asked to leave the ring early because Trifle was upsetting the other ponies. Luckily, Granfer hadn't arrived.

There was a long wait until their next class, so Katy decided to work Trifle in the empty part of the field which was used as an exercise area. Gradually, Trifle became calmer, and Katy felt her relax.

A girl holding an unopened ice-lolly stopped to watch them, so Katy rode over to say hello.

"You're that girl who was on Pure Gold Pets, aren't you? Is this the pony who won the medal?" the girl asked. As if in answer, Trifle lowered her head and blew softly into the girl's hair. "Ah, hello, sweetie-pie!" the girl exclaimed.

"Yes, this is Trifle. I'm just trying to calm..." Katy's answer was cut short by a high-pitched squeaking noise as the girl blew into her ice cream wrapper to loosen it. Alarmed by the strange sound, Trifle wheeled round and galloped off towards the nearest horses she could see — leaving Katy sitting on the ground, wondering what had happened.

The nearest horses were the two-year-old hunter fillies and geldings who were lining up for the final judging of their class in the main ring. Melanie's filly, Dancing Queen, was first in the line-up. Trifle was overjoyed to find a horse she knew. She circled the main ring at a gallop, bucking and squealing with delight. The two-year-olds were only too glad to follow Trifle's bad example, and Dancing Queen definitely lived up to her name. The orderly line-up disintegrated into chaos. Trifle was caught and led away. This made Dancing Queen behave so badly that she had to leave the ring too. Katy was mortified.

After disrupting the whole show, Trifle calmed down and behaved herself. Katy and Trifle left Exford Show with three rosettes from the Exmoor pony classes: third for junior handler, second for novice ridden and first — with a trophy — for junior ridden. Granfer was delighted. Katy's delight was diminished by the knowledge that she had ruined the day for Melanie, who had been so kind to her. Melanie was very nice about it but, in a way, that made it worse — especially as Melanie was going to transport Trifle and Katy to Dunster Show on Friday.

Dunster Show — the largest on Exmoor — is held on Dunster Castle Lawns, with the castle providing a magnificent backdrop.

The Stonyford lorry arrived soon after the gates opened, because Katy and Trifle were entered in one of the first classes of the day. The class was for in-hand registered Exmoor mares of four years old or over, with or without a foal at foot.

"Beats me why the Exmoor pony classes are so early in the morning," Granfer grumbled as he walked to the ringside with Katy. "Exmoors are our native breed, and yet most of their classes are over by the time the crowds arrive."

After Trifle's performance on arriving at Exford Show, Katy was secretly very glad that there weren't many people around. However, her fears were unfounded; Trifle behaved like a true professional, and was placed third out of ten.

"Well done, my girl! You're both getting the hang of this showing lark at last, eh?" Granfer said, beaming with pleasure, as Katy led Trifle out of the ring.

To Katy's surprised delight, Trifle was placed first in the other class she had been entered in that day, which was for ridden Exmoor mares, stallions and geldings of four years and over.

Afterwards, Trifle was taken back to the Stonyford lorry for a well-deserved rest, and then Katy and Alice went off to explore the showground and buy some lunch. After much thought, they decided to buy beef burgers. Katy bit into hers, and a dollop of onions mixed with ketchup squirted down her white show shirt and cream-coloured jodhpurs.

"Eeek!" squealed Katy

"Oh, Katy! Trust you!" Alice giggled. "It's just as well you haven't got any more classes today!"

They were trying to clean up the worst of the mess with napkins from the stall when Sally came running up.

"Thank goodness I've found you, Katy! You're in the championship! It's just been called to the collecting ring! Hurry!"

"What championship, Mum?" Katy asked through a mouthful of burger.

"The ridden mountain and moorland championship, of course! Did no one tell you about it? The first and second prize-winners from all the ridden mountain and moorland classes are entered. Do hurry! Ugh! What on earth is that on your jods?"

Katy blushed, feeling like a complete idiot. "My burger didn't behave itself very well," she said. She made the mistake of looking at Alice, and they both collapsed into helpless laughter.

"It looks as if the burger isn't the only one!" Sally said, looking heavenwards. "Now run, or you'll be late for the championship! Run!"

Somehow, they managed to get ready in time. Alice gave Trifle a quick brush and tacked her up, while Katy changed out of her stained jodhpurs and squeezed into a spare pair belonging to Alice, who was much taller and thinner than Katy. Luckily, Katy's jacket hid the stain on her shirt and the undone popper on the jodhpurs.

As Katy rode into the collecting ring, she felt

unprepared and uncomfortable. Trifle seemed on edge, too, looking warily at the immaculate hindquarters of the dapple grey Connemara pony in front of them.

"Don't worry, Trifle," whispered Katy. "I'm sure a beautiful bottom like that will be much too well-mannered to kick you. We'll never win a prize against this lot, so let's just try to enjoy ourselves."

The rider of the dapple grey turned to talk to a man standing by the collecting ring, and Katy was horrified to see why Trifle was worried. The rider was Val! Katy would be competing against Val in the championship!

Katy was shaking, and she felt sick. Soon, Val would recognise them, and would say something embarrassing in her loud, abrasive voice. There was only one thing they could do — leave the ring before Val realised they were there.

They left the collecting ring unnoticed and headed for the lorries and horse boxes.

"Katy! Wait! What on earth are you doing?"

It was Rachel.

"I'm sorry, but I don't feel well," Katy said.

"Oh, you poor thing! You look terrible — as if you've seen a ghost!" Rachel exclaimed.

"I have, sort of. Val's in the championship

class. I can't go in that class with her there, Rachel! Please don't make me!"

"Of course I won't make you, Katy, but can't you see that this is your big chance?"

"What do you mean?"

"Well, win or lose, this is your big chance to show Val that she can't intimidate you and you'll compete with her on equal terms. You'll be able to prove to her how good Trifle really is. It's an opportunity that's too good to miss, isn't it?"

"Well, I suppose..."

"And just think what it'll be like if you beat her!" Rachel added, smiling up at Katy. "I think you'll kick yourself if you don't go back to that class. You owe it to Trifle."

"Oh, Rachel! You are making me go back, aren't you? I knew you would! Come on, Trifle, we'd better hurry!"

Katy and Trifle returned to the collecting ring with seconds to spare; the competitors were being called in.

The ponies in the class were a funny mixture of shapes and sizes — everything from a Shetland pony on a leading rein to a Highland pony and Val's Connemara, with Trifle somewhere in between. Katy wondered how the judge would be able to compare such varied ponies and pick a winner.

The riders were asked to walk, trot and canter around the ring, following each other. Then they returned to walk and the judge made his preliminary choice as, one by one, the riders were asked to line up in the centre of the ring. This was the bit Katy dreaded. You were supposed to walk round, smiling and pretending you weren't looking at the judge or the steward, but noticing instantly if the steward beckoned to you.

Val was beckoned in first.

The little girl on the Shetland pony was second.

To her delight, Katy was third.

When all the ponies were lined up in the centre of the ring, the judge inspected each one in turn, asked the rider a few questions and then requested an individual show.

Val's show was perfect, as far as Katy could see. Unfortunately, the Shetland was in a bad mood. His ears were back, and he tried to buck as he was led away from the other horses. Katy felt very sorry for his young rider, who smiled bravely although there were tears in her eyes.

It was only when Katy and Trifle stepped out of the line to perform their individual show that Val recognised them. The look of disbelief on her face gave Katy an unusually competitive spirit. She had to show Val how wrong she had been about Trifle.

Katy's energy and determination was picked up by Trifle; she did a fantastic display, with pricked ears and faultless paces.

"What a lovely pony! I bet you have a lot of fun on her, don't you?" the judge said when Katy had finished.

"Yes, Sir!" Katy said, beaming.

Most of the individual shows seemed faultless. How on earth would the judge make his final decision?

The riders were sent to walk round the ring again. Katy's heart was pounding. She knew Trifle had done her best, and that was all that mattered. Val would win — there was no question — but it would be wonderful to be in the first five.

Granfer, Rachel, Sally, Phil, Melanie and Alice were standing at the ringside. Katy couldn't resist making a funny face at them as she rode past, but they didn't laugh and smile; they pointed frantically at the centre of the ring.

"Look at the steward, Katy!" Rachel hissed.

"Concentrate!" Sally said.

Katy looked at the steward. He seemed to be

beckoning her, but she didn't know why. Perhaps Trifle was slightly lame or something. Her heart sank as she rode to the steward.

"Congratulations, Miss! You've won the championship!" the steward said to Katy. "Could you please stand over there, starting a line in the same way as before?"

Katy thought she must be dreaming. "Are you sure?" she squeaked.

"Yes, the judge has made his final decision, Miss. No doubt about it," the steward replied, smiling at her.

Katy took up her place. She was bursting with pride. Out of the corner of her eye she could see her family and friends hugging each other and jumping up and down. Katy knew it wasn't very professional, but she was so delighted that she leant forward and flung her arms round Trifle's neck, giving her a big hug. As she did so, she felt the seat of her jodhpurs start to rip, so she sat up quickly.

Val was called in second, and soon her pony was standing next to Trifle. Katy avoided looking at Val, but she could feel rage radiating from her like heat from a fire.

As she cantered round the ring in a lap of honour, Katy's vision was blurred by tears of joy.

This had to be the proudest moment of her life. Granfer, Rachel, Sally, Phil, Melanie and Alice were at the ringside waiting for her. Trifle was patted, hugged and kissed.

Katy laughed. "She must be wondering what all the fuss is about," she said. "She went round in circles for hours at camp and no one gave her a rosette or made a fuss of her. Here, she just had to do a few laps of the ring and a little show, and we're all over her."

"Yes, humans are most peculiar, aren't they?" Alice said, giving Trifle yet another hug.

"Shh!" said Melanie.

The sound of Val's rasping voice could be heard above the general showground noise. She was telling the judge that he was not fit to judge mountain and moorland ponies, and she proceeded to list the championships her pony had won during the past year.

"If she's won all of those, she shouldn't be entering local shows!" Granfer commented.

"Hush! Listen!" Rachel said.

The judge, red in the face from suppressed fury, had at last managed to interrupt Val. "If you must know, Madam, the reason I chose the Exmoor mare over your pony is that the Exmoor is an excellent example of her breed and she was brimming with character. Furthermore, she looked as if she was really enjoying herself; there was a wonderful partnership between the pony and her rider. I thought your pony gave a very polished performance, but there was no joy in it. He gave the impression he was working for you because he had to, not because he wanted to."

"I have never been so insulted in all my life! I will make an official complaint!" Val shouted. Most of the people in the vicinity had stopped talking and were staring at her, but she didn't notice or didn't care. She flung her rosette onto the ground and stamped on it, then turned and walked away.

"Now that's the sort of person we don't need on Exmoor," said Granfer.

CHAPTER 5
Sharon

After Trifle's success at Dunster Show, Granfer insisted on taking everyone involved — with several other close friends and relations — for a celebratory meal at the pub. Rachel and Mark were invited, of course, and after the meal they announced the good news that they were expecting their first baby. The party became a double celebration, and champagne was ordered. It turned out to be a very expensive night for Granfer.

As they left the pub and walked to their cars, Granfer took Rachel's arm. "Well, what a day this has been!" he said. "A new grandchild, eh? I'm so happy for you, and I thought your mother was going to burst with excitement! She's been feeling a bit down recently, with her arthritis and everything. The prospect of another grandchild will do her no end of good."

"Yes, Mum did look thrilled, didn't she?"

"How about you? This will mean big changes for you, my girl. You won't be able to work all hours at the Exford Stables any more, will you?"

"No, I won't. But if all goes well I'll still be involved in the running of the place. The owners have agreed I can work part-time as the manager if I can find someone to do the routine work. We advertised for a head groom in *Horse and Hound* last week, and so far there have been two replies. We're interviewing people next week."

"Well, you'll be a tough act to follow — that's for certain," Granfer replied.

Sharon Doyle had toothache, and she was sitting in a dentist's waiting room in Tiverton searching through a pile of magazines. Waiting rooms in rural towns like Tiverton often have a few horse magazines hidden between the usual ones about celebrities and fashion. Before long, Sharon found what she was looking for — last week's copy of *Horse and Hound*. She skimmed through the pages and arrived at the section where horses and ponies were advertised for sale. The prices were unbelievable; either the horses were very good or their owners were very optimistic. When Sharon was working at her uncle's horse-dealing yard, the best horses rarely made the price of some of the little ponies advertised in *Horse and Hound*.

Sharon looked at the photos and started to daydream about the horses. She doubted whether any of them would be as good as Comet, a horse she had looked after at her uncle's yard.

Comet had been the best. Sharon had pleaded with her uncle to let her keep the horse, but he'd said they had to shift him quickly because he was a bit hot. "A bit hot" was the term her uncle used for stolen horses; he used the term a lot.

She remembered the day when an elegant lady and two young girls in a very smart lorry had driven into the yard. Sharon had hated them because she knew they had come to try Comet, but she hated them even more because they looked so wealthy and superior. They were dressed in expensive-looking riding clothes, and the girls kept staring at her. She was sure they were giggling behind her back at her dyed red hair and the rings and studs all over her face. They had pretended they were interested in buying Comet, and had taken him out for a ride. Sharon had gone up to her room to cry, because she was sure they would buy him and she would never see him again. In fact, they were friends of Comet's real owner, and they were setting a trap for Sharon's uncle. Soon the place was swarming with police, her uncle was arrested and Comet was loaded into the very smart lorry. Sharon had seen it all from her bedroom window. She still had nightmares about that lorry; it was royal blue with a white stripe along the side and STONYFORD RIDING STABLES in bold writing.

Sharon's uncle had been in prison for half a year now, and Sharon had been without a job for the same length of time. She was living in a hostel with no job, no boyfriend, no qualifications, hardly any money and toothache. Her mum was dead, and she had never known her dad. Sharon loved horses and wanted to work with them, but getting a job as a groom seemed as likely as marrying Prince William.

The dentist was running late. Sharon finished looking at the advertisements for horses and ponies, and went on to the job vacancies. Predictably, the advertisements were for people with experience and qualifications, and they seemed to be miles away — places like Northamptonshire, Surrey and Warwickshire. At the bottom of the page, one advertisement grabbed her attention:

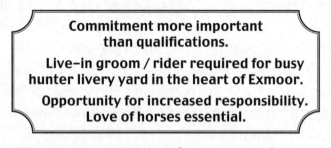

Commitment more important than qualifications.

Live–in groom / rider required for busy hunter livery yard in the heart of Exmoor.

Opportunity for increased responsibility. Love of horses essential.

"Have you got a piece of paper I can borrow?" Sharon asked the receptionist.

"Here you are, dear," said the receptionist, handing Sharon a piece of paper with smiley faces all over it and "Mintyfresh for Miles of Smiles" written along the top.

"Thanks a lot," said Sharon. She copied the telephone number at the bottom of the advertisement onto the smiley paper and put it into her pocket just before the dentist called her into his surgery.

In the afternoon — once the numbness in her mouth had worn off — Sharon collected some coins together, went to a public telephone and rang the number on the smiley paper.

That call changed the course of her life.

Rachel was not in a good mood. She was feeling tired and sick. Morning sickness seemed to strike at any time of day with her. It was four o'clock in the afternoon. She had interviewed two girls for the job at the Exford stables, and they had both turned it down, saying that the accommodation was not good enough. Rachel had been rather relieved because she hadn't liked either of the girls very much. All her hopes now rested on the third, and final, girl who had applied for the job. She had telephoned the previous afternoon, and had said that she didn't have a car but she would come by public transport. Rachel had pointed out that bus services to Exford were infrequent, but that hadn't deterred the girl. "I'll get there somehow," she'd said. "Please wait for me. I'd really love the job."

At half past five, Rachel decided to give up waiting. She was locking the tack room door when a small, thin girl who looked like a new-age traveller walked into the yard. The girl had short, dyed black hair, tatty old jeans, a misshapen sweater, trainers and a grey canvas rucksack.

The most striking thing about her was the studs and rings all over her face.

"I'm sorry, you can't come in here. It's a private yard, you see," Rachel said.

The girl looked rather taken aback. "Oh, I am sorry," she said, with a lilting Irish accent. "I'm looking for someone called Rachel Bowden."

"That's me. Who are you?" Rachel asked, still on her guard.

"I'm Sharon Doyle. I've come about the job. I'm sorry I'm so late, but I had to walk from Dulverton."

Rachel's heart sank. It occurred to her that she could say the job was taken, but she felt she had to at least give the girl a cup of tea, especially since she had made such an effort to get there.

Sharon could see that Rachel was appalled by her appearance. She wished she could magic away all the rings and studs. Daring face-piercing had impressed her ex-boyfriend, but it wasn't impressing Rachel. Sharon hadn't eaten for 24 hours, she had spent all her money on transport, and her feet ached. She was miles from home — if you could call the hostel home — and she had nowhere to stay the night. She felt like crying.

"Come into the tack room and have a cup of tea," Rachel said.

Sharon drew in a deep breath as she entered the tack room. "Mmm! I love the smell of tack rooms," she said. "Oh, wow! I've never seen one with lots of books in it before! Awesome! Mark Rashid, Monty Roberts, Kelly Marks, Pat Parelli .... Their ideas about how to handle horses are so inspirational. I could sit here and read for ever!"

Rachel was surprised and pleased. "I'm a firm believer in using communication, not force, when working with horses," she said.

"You're so right!" Sharon replied. "I'm really interested in natural horsemanship, and I'd love to learn more about it."

"Well, you've come to the right place, then," Rachel said, warming to the girl. Perhaps she would be worth considering, after all. "Do your family live in Tiverton?"

"No. I was born and raised in Ireland. I never knew my father; it was always just my mother and me. When my mother died three years ago, I moved to Tiverton to live with my uncle. But now he's moved away, so I'm living in a hostel. I've got to get out of there in two months, though, because you can't stay after you're 18. My uncle was a jockey, and he kept a few horses. He taught me how to ride, and I used to ride all sorts of horses for him...."

Once Sharon started talking it was as if the floodgates had opened, although she was careful to avoid telling Rachel that her uncle was in prison for stealing horses.

The more Sharon talked, the more Rachel liked her; although they had led very different lives, they had so much in common. Moon seemed to like Sharon, too. He nuzzled her like an old friend.

"What a lovely horse!" Sharon exclaimed. "In a funny sort of way he reminds me of Comet, a horse we had at the yard."

"Well, he's called Moon. He's sort of mine but someone else owns him, if that doesn't sound daft."

"Not at all," Sharon replied. "I felt that Comet was mine, but it turned out that someone else owned him."

When Rachel showed Sharon the groom's flat above the tack room, Sharon reacted as if it were a castle. In fact, it consisted of a shabby bedroom with second-hand bargain furniture, plus a bathroom with mildew and dodgy plumbing. For Sharon, an added attraction was that the whole place smelt of the tack room below.

"Well, it's yours if you want it," Rachel heard

herself saying.

Sharon couldn't believe her ears. "Are you sure?" she said. "I mean, this is such a smart, well-run place! I look a right mess and I've got no qualifications, you know."

"It's your honesty I admire!" Rachel laughed. "Besides, as the advertisement said, commitment is more important than qualifications. You love horses, you're very committed, and we can work on your appearance and qualifications. So, what do you think?"

"Yes, please!" Sharon said. She sat wearily on the bed and began to cry. "Thank you!" she whispered through her tears. Then she looked at Rachel with puffy, liquid eyes. "Thank you so much! I won't let you down," she said.

Rachel knew she was taking a risk, but her instincts told her that Sharon was trustworthy. She gave her £10 to get a meal in the pub and told her she could stay in the groom's flat for the night. The following day she would drive Sharon to Tiverton to collect her belongings and complete any necessary paperwork.

"Did you find a groom, then?" Mark asked Rachel as they sat down to a hastily prepared supper in their bungalow.

"Yes. She's called Sharon," Rachel replied.

"What's she like?"

"She's got studs all over her face — and probably over the rest of her body, too — dyed black hair, worn out clothes, no qualifications and no references. Oh, and no known relations except an uncle, who seems to have abandoned her for some reason."

"Blimey!" said Mark. "Whatever made you take her on?"

"Feminine intuition," Rachel smiled.

"That's a smart way of saying madness," Mark replied. "She'll stick out like a sore thumb in Exford amongst the tweeds and waxed jackets."

"Well, I think she'll be a breath of fresh air. Exmoor people are very tolerant of eccentrics, especially if they like horses and the country way of life, and she does seem to be a genuinely nice person."

Rachel was right. Sharon worked hard and was eager to learn. After the initial shock waves her appearance created at the stables and in the village, Sharon was accepted for who she was. The owners were delighted by the way she cared for their horses, and Rachel was delighted that she could spend more time at home with Mark.

Sharon was truly happy for the first time in her life. She had never really had a proper family, but now it seemed as if everyone in the village was her family. On her 18th birthday, they had a surprise party for her at the pub and gave her presents. She hadn't had a birthday present for years. Best of all, she was surrounded by horses all the time. She loved all of them, but she loved Moon the most; he was exactly like a bigger, fatter, happier version of Comet.

As time went on, Sharon was allowed to ride Moon. The more she did, the harder it was to fight off an uneasy thought that was lodging in her mind: Moon and Comet were the same horse. They had to be. Comet hadn't had Moon's white moon-shaped mark between his eyes, but Sharon knew her uncle had often used hair dye to mask distinctive markings on stolen horses. Also, he had often changed their names. Rachel had told Sharon that Moon had probably started his COPD problem at a dishonest dealer's yard when Rachel was in Australia. It was all beginning to add up.

How could Sharon tell Rachel that it was her uncle who had treated Moon so badly and had tried to steal him from Mr. Jackson? Rachel would be furious, and Sharon would lose her job.

CHAPTER 6

The Christmas Party

The leaves fell off the trees, and the days became shorter. Almost overnight, the fields became wet and muddy. The land slipped into its annual winter sulk.

Phil and Sally Squires decided to beat the winter blues by having a Christmas party at Barton Farm. Invitations to friends and neighbours were slipped inside the Christmas cards posted in the second week of December. Sally wrote on the top of the invitation to Rachel and Mark, "Do ask Sharon to come. We'd love to meet her."

The new neighbours at Wellsworthy Farm were the first to arrive.

"Come in and have a seat before the hoards arrive," Granfer said. "Sally and Phil are just getting changed. They'll be down in a minute. I don't think you've met my wife, Peggy, have you?" He led the guests into the sitting room. "Peggy, this is Dean and his — um — partner, Barbara. They've moved into Wellsworthy."

"Pleased to meet you," said Gran. "Katy, take Barbara's coat, will you?"

Katy was handed a very expensive fur coat which glistened with raindrops.

"Oh, do call me Babs. Barbara sounds so formal!" Babs squeaked. She had the voice of a little girl, and was dressed in a pink trouser suit — just like a living Barbie doll. "My, what a night! Does it ever stop raining here?"

"Yes, sometimes it snows," Granfer said wryly, handing Babs and Dean their drinks. "How are you getting on at Wellsworthy, then?"

"Er, is that what you locals call it? Wellsery?"

Dean asked. "We call it Wellsworthy."

Granfer chuckled. "It may be spelt Wellsworthy, but here on Exmoor words ending in 'worthy' are pronounced 'ery'. Pinkery Pond is even spelt that way on maps nowadays, although it always used to be spelt Pinkworthy."

"Fascinating. Are there any other weird and wonderful pronunciations we should know about?" Dean replied.

"The most obvious one is Simonsbath, which is pronounced Simmonsbath. You'll get the hang of it all once you've lived here a while," said Granfer.

"Oh, we didn't buy Wellsworthy to live here and farm it!" Babs exclaimed, as if that were the silliest idea in the world. "The plan is to get rid of the land and convert the house and the farm buildings into luxury holiday accommodation. There'll be an indoor swimming pool, gym, games room — the works. It'll be super!"

Granfer wasn't so sure. He had fond memories of Ted Delbridge, who had farmed Wellsworthy all his life but had died the previous spring, leaving no children to take on the farm. Ted had been a good farmer and a wonderful neighbour. Granfer remembered shearing his first sheep in Ted Delbridge's barn.

"Well, we haven't really decided what we're going to do yet," Dean said, giving Babs a stern look.

She carried on, undaunted. " Nonsense! We agreed this was just an investment opportunity! Personally I can't stand it here — always raining and no decent shops for miles. Our main home is in Portugal, you see. I thrive in hot sunshine! Dean calls me his tropical flower, don't you, Darling?"

Dean looked uncomfortable.

"Ooops! Silly me! I always talk too much!" Babs twittered.

Neither Granfer nor Gran could think of anything to say that wouldn't be rude, so they said nothing. There was an awkward silence. Everyone sipped their drinks. They were saved by the arrival of Melanie, Alice and her younger twin brothers, Rupert and Josh.

Katy and Alice went upstairs to Katy's bedroom as soon as they could.

"Phew! Thank goodness you came!" Katy exclaimed. "The people who've moved into Wellsworthy are horrible! They're going to build a swimming pool and all sorts of crazy things in those big old barns."

"Cool! Perhaps we'll be able to use their pool!" said Alice.

"That isn't the point, Alice! They'll destroy Mr. Delbridge's lovely old farm, and it will be another farm lost forever."

"Oh, whatever," said Alice. She didn't really care what happened to Wellsworthy and she certainly didn't want to fall out over it.

Katy changed the subject. "Do you want to see the e-mail Greg sent me the other day? I've kept a copy in my special drawer. Here it is. Look, he's put, 'Have a great Christmas. We're having a serious drought here. Can you send some of your Exmoor rain over? Love from Greg.' He even wrote, 'Love from Greg'! Isn't that great?"

Secretly, Alice thought that Katy was totally unrealistic about Greg. He was Mark's youngest brother: tall, rugged, handsome and — most important — nine years older than Katy, and working in Australia for a couple of years. Any fool could see that Greg looked upon Katy as a little sister, but she idolised him. Alice didn't want to hurt Katy's feelings by saying what she really thought. Instead, she said, "Well, it shows he's very fond of you. He would have put something like 'Best Wishes' otherwise, wouldn't he?"

"You are so right, Alice! Whee! I'm so happy!"

said Katy, dancing round the room.

There was a knock at Katy's bedroom door.

"Katy! Alice! Are you in there?" Sally called. "Can you come down now and start handing the food around? Everyone's arrived at the same time and I'm rushed off my feet."

Sharon was nervous about going to a party full of people she didn't know. She was even more nervous when she arrived with Rachel and Mark and saw how many people were there. She stayed close to Rachel and listened to the conversations going on around her.

"When's the baby due, Rachel? The end of March? You won't be much help to Mark at lambing time, then! Ha! Ha!" said a large, red-faced man.

"What a wet autumn it's been! I'm sure we're having more rain than we used to. The weather seems to be intent on breaking one record after another nowadays," said a thin, rather nervous woman.

"Don't want a sheepdog puppy, do you? I've got two bitches left from a litter of seven. Both parents are good workers," said another large, red-faced man.

"Hello, Rachel! I haven't seen you for ages —

in fact, not since that wonderful day at Dunster Show. You look radiant! How are you feeling? Is morning sickness a thing of the past now?" asked a very smart, attractive lady.

Sharon turned her head away. Her heart was racing.

Rachel smiled. "Hello, Melanie! Yes, I'm feeling fine now. Melanie, this is Sharon — the wonderful new groom at the stables. Sharon, meet Melanie — expert horsewoman and owner of Stonyford Riding Stables."

Melanie looked stunned.

Sharon gulped. "Yes, I know. We've met before."

"Oh? Where?" Rachel asked.

Sharon did not know what to say.

Melanie broke the silence. "Sharon was working as a groom at the stables we rescued Moon from, weren't you, Sharon?" Then she added, with a smile, "I remember you because you rode beautifully."

"This is unbelievable!" Rachel exclaimed. "Is it true, Sharon? Is your uncle the dealer who was sent to prison for horse theft?"

Sharon looked at the ground. "Yes, he is. I'm so sorry, Rachel."

"Did you know that Moon was at Exford

Stables, then? Is that why you came? To take him away?"

"No! No, I swear I didn't realise that the horse I'd known as Comet was your horse, Moon! I wanted the job at the stables because I wanted to work with horses, and the job sounded ideal — commitment more important than qualifications, and somewhere to live, too. Please believe me, Rachel!" Sharon said.

"So when did you realise your Comet was, in fact, Moon?" Rachel asked more calmly.

"I got the idea he might be, fairly early on; but it wasn't until I rode him that I knew for certain. Horses like Moon don't turn up very often," Sharon replied.

"Why on earth didn't you tell me?"

"Oh, Rachel! I'm so sorry! Please don't be angry! I've been so happy at the stables, and I was afraid I'd lose my job."

"Well, I must admit I'm really disappointed in you, Sharon," Rachel said.

"I know. Thank you for everything, Rachel. You gave me a chance, and I blew it. Don't worry; I'll leave tomorrow morning," Sharon said, turning to leave the room.

"Hang on a minute! I'm disappointed in you because you thought I'd be angry with you for telling me the truth. The truth is that you did nothing wrong. It wasn't your fault that your uncle was a crook. I'm certainly not going to give the best groom on Exmoor the sack over a little misunderstanding. Promise me one thing, though."

"Anything," Sharon said.

"No more secrets. If something's bothering you — or you think there's something I ought to know — you come and tell me about it."

"I promise. No more secrets," Sharon said emphatically.

Dean and Babs were the first to arrive and the last to leave. Finally, they said goodbye to their hosts.

Babs was very drunk. "Isn't it a hoot? Dean is going to go horseback riding with that woman from Stoneybroke, or whatever it's called. What's her name? Lemony?"

"She's called Melanie," Dean corrected her, looking embarrassed.

"Ah, yes! Well, I think it's sweet of him, don't you? When in Rome, do as the Romans and all that! Hi-Yo, Silver! Away! Neigh!" Babs pretended to canter to their black Range Rover like a prancing horse.

"I do apologise. She's had rather a lot to drink. I hope we haven't outstayed our welcome. Thank you very much for a great party. Happy Christmas!" Dean said, as politely as he could while hurrying after Babs. She lost her footing on the sloping concrete and — before Dean could catch her — she fell against the car, setting off the burglar alarm. It made a fearsome noise.

"Ah, the peace and quiet of the countryside!" Babs yelled above the din, then she screeched with laughter at her own joke.

At last, Dean managed to turn off the alarm and get Babs into the car. The Range Rover drove off down the lane, and Barton Farm was left in peace.

It rained heavily on Christmas Day. Katy took a small plastic bottle, washed it thoroughly and filled it with pure rainwater from Barton Farm. She wrapped it well and, a couple of days after Christmas, she posted the bottle to Greg in Australia. Nancy in the Post Office was puzzled by the customs label Katy stuck to the parcel:

> **Description of goods:** *rain (gift)*
> **Value of contents:** *priceless*

CHAPTER 7

Home Alone

Katy checked the post and her e-mails every day, expecting news that Greg had received his unusual Christmas present, but there was no word from him.

At the end of January, Katy's parents went to London for a week. Some of Phil's paintings had been chosen for a special exhibition of modern landscape artists in a smart London gallery, so he planned to combine a business trip with a holiday. He and Sally had not been on holiday together since their honeymoon.

They left on a cold, wet Sunday morning.

"Goodbye, Darling," Sally said to Katy. "I've put a note on the table to remind you about everything you'll have to do. The fridge is well-stocked and there's lots of food in the freezer. Make your packed lunch for school the night before, and store it in the fridge. Tom will take you down to the bus stop, won't you, Tom?"

Tom nodded.

"Take care of each other, now. Remember, we're only a phone call away," Sally said, hugging Katy and Tom in turn.

Phil kissed Katy and gave Tom a fatherly pat on the shoulder. "Bye, Tom. Remember to check the cows regularly — one or two are very close to calving. Oh, and please fence round those silage bales in Moor Field. I'm sorry to go on about it, but you really should have done it in the autumn. It's an accident waiting to happen."

"Yeah, yeah, Dad. I said I'll do it, and I'll do it — OK?" Tom said.

"Well, make sure you do. Good luck with everything, both of you, and no silly arguments! Granfer will come round tomorrow at breakfast time," Phil said. Then he and Sally got into the car and drove off, waving.

To begin with, Katy thought that being alone with Tom was great. They made toasted sandwiches for lunch and ate them in the sitting room, watching television. Sally never allowed her family to eat in the sitting room.

There was a good film on television, and they watched all of it. Afterwards, it was a mad dash to get all the livestock fed and watered before nightfall. At least there were no stables to muck out; neither Jacko nor Trifle were clipped, so they did not have to be stabled at night. When all the farm work was done, Katy still had her homework to do.

"We'll have a proper fry-up for tea," Tom said. "I'll cook and you can wash up."

By the time Katy had finished her homework, she was too tired to wash all the dirty dishes and greasy, charred pans in the sink.

Katy overslept on Monday morning. She raced downstairs, and there was no one there. Tom was out working on the farm, apparently unaware that he was supposed to drive Katy to the bus stop.

There was no time for breakfast, and Katy had forgotten to make a packed lunch. She grabbed her school bag and ran down the lane. The bus stop was almost a mile away, and she arrived in the nick of time. A friend gave Katy a sandwich and a bit of chocolate at lunch time but, apart from that, she had nothing to eat all day. Tom was not at the bus stop after school, so Katy had to walk home in the rain. She was cold, hungry and miserable.

Tom did not have a good day, either. When he went out to the cow shed at 6.30 in the morning, he found a cow lying on her side with a very weak newborn calf on the straw behind her. It looked as if the cow had been struggling to give birth for a long time and, now that her ordeal was over, she could not summon the energy to get up and take care of her baby. It was her first calf, and it was huge. Tom felt very guilty; he should have checked the cows in the middle of the night, but he hadn't bothered. The calf was cold and wet. Tom rubbed it with straw and gave the cow a drink of water and some silage. Then he placed the calf by the cow's head, and left them to get to know each other while he set about the early morning farm work. Too late, he remembered about Katy and the school bus. He dashed back to the house, but she had gone.

While Tom was having his breakfast, Granfer

walked into the house. His eyebrows went up when he saw the dirty dishes stacked in the sink.

"I know what you're going to say, Granfer," Tom said. "It's OK — I'll clear everything up in a minute. A heifer had a difficult calving early this morning — a great big bull calf — and it's put me behind with everything."

"Did you manage to calve her down by yourself? You should have called me, you know. I don't mind coming out at any time of the night or day if there's a problem."

"I know, Granfer, but I didn't need help. Everything's fine now," Tom said. He was keen to close the subject before any more questions were asked.

"Was the calf all right?"

"Yes."

"And sucking from its mum OK?"

"Yup," Tom said, avoiding Granfer's keen gaze. He had forgotten to check that, but he would after breakfast.

"Need any help with anything?"

"No thanks, Granfer. I can manage."

"Well, if you're sure," Granfer said doubtfully. "Ring me if you need me, won't you?"

"I will. Thanks."

"Is Katy OK?"

"Yes, she's fine."

"Good. I'll be off, then."

"Bye, Granfer."

The calf had not drunk any milk from his mother. Lack of oxygen during birth had made him rather dopey. He wandered around aimlessly, occasionally bumping into things and trying half-heartedly to suck from them. His mother followed him wherever he went. She seemed afraid to take her eyes off her new baby. Every time he wandered near the teats between her hind legs, she turned to face him, mooing lovingly and licking him so hard he nearly fell over. She seemed to be unaware that if her calf did not drink milk soon, he would die.

Tom caught the cow and tied her up, and then guided the calf to the cow's udder. The calf was surprisingly strong, and fought Tom every step of the way. The cow became very upset because she thought Tom was trying to hurt her baby. What Tom really needed was another pair of hands, but his pride wouldn't allow him to contact Granfer and ask for help — not after he had told Granfer that the calf had been sucking from its mother.

It took Tom three hours to get the calf feeding

properly. The whole process tested his strength, skill and patience to the full, but he was rewarded by the knowledge that he had, in the end, saved the calf's life. He wished Granfer had been there to see it.

Tom had intended to fence around the silage bales in Moor Field that afternoon, but by the time he had dealt with the cow and calf, bedded up the cows in the shed with fresh straw and fed the animals in the fields, it was getting dark and raining hard. As Tom drove the tractor into the yard, he saw a bedraggled figure walking towards the house. It was Katy; Tom had forgotten about the school bus.

CHAPTER 8
Midnight Feast

That night, one of the Exmoor mares from the herd on the Common rubbed her saturated, itchy winter coat against the gate separating the Common from Moor Field. Suddenly, the gate hook jolted out of its lodging and the gate flew open. The Barton herd of Exmoor ponies poured into Moor Field like water bursting through a dam. First they ate the long, wet grass; then they found the silage bales — full of sweet, rich silage. The ponies had a tremendous midnight feast. They ripped at the plastic wrapping around the bales to get at the delicious contents, and moved from bale to bale in a feeding frenzy.

Jacko and Trifle were in the field next door. They trotted to the gate to see what all the fuss was about. Peter Pan, the stallion, went over to greet them, and much squealing and kicking followed. Trifle leant all her weight against the gate; opening gates by pushing against them was one of the tricks Katy had taught her. Eventually, the gate restraining the two ponies broke with a crash, and they galloped through to join the herd of Exmoors. There was a bit of a scuffle between Jacko and Peter Pan, but the gelding soon gave way to the stallion and kept away from him. All the ponies settled down to the serious business of feasting on the silage.

On Tuesday morning, Tom made sure he woke Katy in good time and drove her to the school bus, and Katy made sure she remembered her lunch. Giving Katy a lift to the bus made Tom late with the farm work. It was 11 o'clock when he set off on the quad bike to check over the farm. By that time, the ponies had been in Moor Field for nearly 12 hours. A scene of devastation greeted Tom as he drove into Moor Field.

There was no time to lose. Grass is preserved in silage bales because air is kept out by the plastic wrapping — like food is preserved in tins.

As soon as the wrapping is damaged and air gets into the silage, it starts to go bad. Tom herded the ponies out onto the Common, noticing that Jacko and Trifle were amongst them only when they were galloping off across the moor.

Rachel's husband, Mark, had silage-making equipment which he hired out to other farmers during the summer. For the past few years, he had helped with the silage harvest at Barton Farm. Tom rushed back to the house and dialled Mark's number.

"Mark? Oh, thank goodness you're there! I've got a bit of an emergency. Is your bale wrapper handy? Well, can you get it out of winter storage? No, I haven't gone mad. Those damned ponies broke in from the Common and shredded the bales in Moor Field. No, I didn't put a fence round the bales. Yes, I know I should have, but I just never got around to it. You can? Cheers! I'll see you in a couple of hours."

Tom and Mark spent the afternoon re-wrapping silage bales and putting a temporary fence around them. As they finished, Mark spotted Trifle and Jacko standing expectantly at the Common gate.

"Are those ponies Jacko and Trifle?" Mark asked.

"Oh, yes, they are! Thank goodness for that!" Tom replied. "They went out with the herd this morning, and I didn't have time to get them back. Give me a hand to get them in, will you? We'll have to put them in a different field because they broke that gate down, the little vandals! Life would be so much simpler without ponies."

"Well, at least they keep the girls happy!" Mark said.

"Life would be a lot simpler without girls, too!" Tom said, smiling. Then his smile turned to a frown, and he looked at his watch. "Damn! I've forgotten to pick up Katy again! Not a word to her about all this, please, Mark. Not a word to anyone!"

"Don't worry, your secret is safe with me. Are you coming to the skittles match at Molland on Thursday night?"

"I can't. I promised Mum and Dad I wouldn't leave Katy alone in the house at night," Tom said.

"How about getting Sharon to baby-sit? I'm sure she could do with a bit of extra cash. I could drive her over here and pick you up at the same time. You need some time off; farming can be a lonely old business."

"OK," said Tom. "If Sharon can be with Katy, I'll come. Thanks, Mark."

At supper that night Katy asked, "Why was Uncle Mark here with the silage wrapper?"

"How do you know he was?"

"I saw him drive past my bedroom window."

"Some bales had rat damage, so I had to re-wrap them," Tom said.

"Dad used to patch up rat holes with silage tape. Why did you bother to re-wrap the bales?"

"They were big rats."

"Oh."

On Thursday night, Mark took Sharon to Barton Farm and picked up Tom.

Sharon walked into the kitchen at Barton Farm and exclaimed, "Ugh! Gross! Don't you ever do any washing-up?"

"No," Tom said cheerfully as he was leaving. "But we'll have to soon because we're running out of clean dishes. Bye, then, you girls. Be good!"

"Right!" Sharon said to Katy. "I'll wash, and you can dry everything and put it away."

"But Tom made most of this mess! I don't see why I should clear up all his dirty dishes!" Katy complained.

"Well, I'm not responsible for any of this washing-up, but I'm going to do it because it needs to be done," said Sharon. "If you don't want to help, that's fine. Go and watch TV or something."

Katy knew she could not leave Sharon to do the washing-up while she did nothing, so she took a cloth from the drawer and walked over to the sink.

Soon, the girls were chatting like old friends.

"When's your mum coming back?" Sharon asked.

"Sunday lunchtime."

"She can't come home to a mess. If I can get a lift over here on Sunday morning, I'll come and help you tidy up before she gets home."

"Could you, Sharon? That would be great!" Katy said. "Somehow, housework isn't as bad when there's two of us; it seems so impossible by myself. I'm beginning to realise how much work Mum does. Will you be offended if I tell you something?"

Sharon looked amused. "Why do people ask that before they say something really offensive? Go on."

"When Alice and I first saw you at your uncle's yard in Tiverton, we thought you were really, um, well, weird — and rather grumpy, too. But I like you a lot now. I wish I had a big sister like you."

"I wouldn't mind a little sister like you, either, Katy Squires!" said Sharon, flicking a dishcloth at her. "And will you be offended if I tell you something?"

"Why do people ask that before they say something really offensive? Go on!" Katy replied, mimicking Sharon's Irish accent.

"When I saw you for the first time, I thought you were a stuck-up snob, with that posh lorry and your fancy riding gear," said Sharon. "It just goes to show that you shouldn't judge people by their appearance, eh?"

True to her word, Sharon went to Barton Farm on Sunday morning to help Katy clean the house. With Sharon there, Tom decided to help with the housework, too. When they had finished the housework, they all went down to the farmyard and tidied that up as well. Working with Sharon made any job seem easier.

Sally and Phil were delighted to see how clean and tidy everything was on their return.

"We'll have to go away more often!" Sally said.

"Please don't!" Katy replied. Life was much easier when packed lunches, lifts to the bus, clean clothes and washing-up just happened — like magic.

CHAPTER 9
The Lesson

From then on, Sharon spent a lot of her spare time at Barton Farm. The Squires family began to wonder how they had managed without her. She helped Sally in the house, Tom on the farm and Katy with Trifle and Jacko.

Every day, Katy checked her e-mails, and she was always disappointed because there was no message from Greg. In the middle of February, she plucked up the courage to send him an e-mail asking if he had received his Christmas present, because it could have been lost in the post. There was no reply, and Katy did not dare to send another in case he thought she was being a pest. Sending a bottle of water to Greg had seemed like a brilliant idea at the time. Katy had been so sure he would love it, but it was becoming increasingly obvious that his silence meant he thought the present was too silly for words. Self-doubt gnawed at Katy. Greg was the most wonderful person in the world, and she had ruined their friendship by sending a ridiculous plastic bottle of water halfway round the world to him. How could she have been so stupid?

In March, the vet said that Jacko could be shod and ridden on soft ground. Sharon and Katy decided to go out for a ride together. Katy had become so used to Trifle's round body, bushy mane and short, quick strides, that it felt really strange to be riding Jacko again.

Sharon got the giggles when she trotted on Trifle for the first time. "This is like riding a sewing machine!" she said.

Katy laughed. "Yes, it is a bit, isn't it? I'm going to jump this branch here, Sharon, but you'd better go around it. Trifle's scared of jumping."

Jacko jumped the branch with ease. He seemed delighted to be out working again. Katy glanced behind her just in time to see Trifle leaping over the branch with her ears pricked, giving Jacko a rumbling whinny as if to say, "Wait for me!"

"Wow! A jumping sewing machine! She must have been so eager to keep up with Jacko, she forgot to be scared," said Sharon.

The girls were riding over the Common when they met Melanie and Dean. Melanie was riding Max, her chestnut hunter, and Dean was on Major, the most dependable horse at Stonyford. Katy was amused to see that Major was on a leading rein; it was funny to see an adult being led. One look at Dean's riding style showed it was a wise precaution. His toes pointed downwards, which tipped his body forwards so that he had to steady himself by gripping the pommel of the saddle with his hands. This gave him no control over the reins, which hung loosely like skipping ropes.

"Howdee, Pardners! Whadda ya think?" Dean said in a mock American drawl.

Katy stifled a giggle. She thought Dean was the worst rider she had ever seen.

"I think you're taming that mustang just fine, cowboy. But you'll find it a heck of a lot easier to stay upright if you keep your heels down," Melanie said tactfully.

"Yes, Ma'am!" Dean said, sitting up in the saddle and saluting. He nearly overbalanced, and saved himself from falling off by grabbing the pommel of the saddle again. "Are all horsy women as bossy as you, Ma'am?"

"Listen, Sunshine," Melanie said, smiling. "If you want a riding lesson, I'll give you one, but if you want someone to massage your ego and tell you you're wonderful, you've got the wrong person."

"I love it when you're assertive!" Dean teased.

"Melanie isn't bossy! She's the best riding teacher in the world!" Katy said.

"Thank you, Katy! I need a bit of moral support. Why are adults so much more difficult to teach than children?" Melanie said. "Hello, Sharon. Nice to see you! How are you getting on with Trifle?"

Sharon felt tongue-tied. It was the first time she had seen Melanie since the Christmas party. "OK, thanks," she said.

"More than OK!" Katy said. "Guess what? Sharon jumped Trifle over a fallen branch, and she cleared it brilliantly!"

"That's great news," said Melanie. "It's lovely to see Jacko out and about again. How is he?"

"He seems fine, thanks," said Katy.

"Now you'll have two ponies to ride."

"I know. I would like Trifle to have a year off to breed a foal, but I don't know what Tom and Dad will say about the prospect of three ponies at the farm."

"To a casual observer, it seems that Exmoor women are dangerously addicted to collecting horses!" Dean said.

Melanie smiled. "Sadly, it's an affliction with no known cure."

"How about making it illegal for women to have money? That would cure it," Dean said.

"That would be a mild deterrent, but not a cure. We'd soon find a way around that!" Melanie said, laughing. "Come on, cowboy. I've got to get back to the ranch in time for the two-thirty ride. Bye, Katy. Bye, Sharon."

When Melanie and Dean were out of hearing distance, Katy said, "Crikey! Isn't Dean a terrible rider?"

"I expect you were once, too. I think he's very brave to have a go," Sharon said.

Katy wished she had kept her mouth shut.

CHAPTER 10

Out of the Blue

Rachel and Mark had a baby daughter on 28th March. They called her Heather. When Rachel and Heather were back from the hospital, Sally took Katy to visit them.

It was a really weird experience. Rachel's house was different. It smelt of baby things, and it was clean and tidy — not a muddy girth in sight. Rachel was different, too — strangely soft and motherly, and wearing a dressing gown rather than her usual jeans and polo shirt. Katy felt very out of place, and wasn't sure what to do or say. In contrast, Sally was in her element, talking about hospitals, nappies and babies. Heather started to cry. It was a loud, demanding cry. Sally picked her up and gave her a cuddle.

"You were once this size, Katy," Sally said. "Oh, I do love babies! Here you are, Rachel. I think she needs a feed."

Katy found it impossible to believe that she had ever been like the tiny, pink, helpless, squirming bundle lying in Rachel's arms. One thing was for certain: she would never have a baby. Other baby animals, like foals and lambs, were much more fun.

Rachel smiled at Katy. "Mark and I have a very special favour to ask you, Katy," she said. "Will you be Heather's godmother? Sharon's going to be her other godmother, and Greg's agreed to be her godfather."

Katy was speechless. She stared at Rachel with her mouth open, like a goldfish. She was astonished and flattered by Rachel's request, but it was the mention of Greg's name which really took her by surprise.

"How is Greg? Still in New Zealand?" Sally asked.

"No, he arrived back in Australia yesterday. All right for some, eh? Nine months work and then three months play. He telephoned this morning. It sounds as if he had a great holiday. Oh, and he loved the water you sent him, Katy! What a brilliant present! He drank a toast to Heather with it while he was on the telephone, and he said it was better than any champagne."

Two weeks later, a large parcel arrived for Katy from Australia. It contained a huge, cuddly toy kangaroo and a postcard of a Merino sheep. On the back of the postcard, Greg had written, "Happy Birthday — well, I'm posting this on your birthday! I'm not as good at presents as you are, but I hope you like Katy the Kangaroo! Her baby (called a joey) is stuck inside the pouch with Velcro. I'm coming home for Heather's christening in December. See you then. Love, Greg."

The kangaroo had pride of place on Katy's bed, and she read the postcard several times a day for the next few weeks. She felt as if she were walking on air. She wished she could talk to Alice about everything, but Alice's father had taken her and her twin brothers — together with his new wife — to the Bahamas for the whole of the Easter holidays.

Katy's mission for the holidays was to persuade Tom to let her put Trifle in foal. She knew she had to pick her moment wisely, and at last the right one came along. Lambing was nearly over, it was a sunny spring day and Tom, Sharon and Katy were having a cup of tea in the kitchen.

"I was thinking of putting Trifle in foal this year, now that I can ride Jacko again," Katy said casually.

"Good idea. She can run with the herd out on the Common, and that will be one less pony on the farm," said Tom. "She'll have her freedom, and I'll have my grass. Ideal!"

Why is it that when you really dread something, it often turns out to be much easier than expected? Katy thought.

As usual, the Exmoor Pony Society Stallion Parade and Annual General Meeting was held on the first Wednesday in May. But this year was special, because Granfer was going to receive a presentation for his outstanding service to the Society, so Katy was allowed the day off school to accompany him.

"What happens at the Stallion Parade, Granfer?" Katy asked as they drove across Exmoor.

"Well, I suppose the main point is that all the stallions which are available for breeding can be shown to any interested Exmoor pony owners, and it's also a chance for young stallions to be inspected for a license to breed. Good-quality stallions whose owners are willing to receive other mares for breeding are awarded a premium."

"What's a premium?"

"Money."

"Why didn't we bring Peter Pan, then? We could have made some money!"

Granfer chuckled. "If you fancy catching him, taking him away from his mares, loading him into a horsebox and then leading him round a show ring with other stallions — when he hasn't been handled since he was a yearling — you're welcome to, my girl! Mind you, in the old days that's exactly what people did. Then, most of the stallions were unhandled and living with their herds on the moor. There were some fun and games at the Stallion Parade in those days, and no mistake! It was more like a rodeo than a parade, with several strong men hanging on to each stallion. Nowadays, most of the stallions are well-handled show ponies kept in fields and stables. Yes, it's certainly a very tame affair now, in comparison. Still, it's useful to see what's about. I'll be looking for a new stallion to run with our mares next year, and I happen to know that Mrs. Soames is taking a very nice two year-old colt to be inspected for a license today."

It is not a good idea to let closely related animals breed with each other, so Granfer always changed his herd stallion every three years. Mrs. Soames was an old friend who bred Exmoors on a farm near Withypool. She was a straightforward, no nonsense woman with a heart of gold and an encyclopaedic knowledge of Exmoor ponies. Katy thought she was wonderful.

"Oh, good. I'd like to see Mrs. Soames again," Katy said.

Katy had a lovely morning, surrounded by Exmoor ponies and friendly people. She had no idea about the surprise Granfer was planning for her in the afternoon.

At the end of the AGM, a presentation was made to Granfer. He made a short speech of thanks before saying, "I'm so glad that my granddaughter, Katy, is with me today. I would like you all to know that I am giving the Barton herd to her. They'll be Katy's ponies from now on. I know that in her capable hands, the future of the Barton herd will be assured, and the long-standing relationship between the Squires family and the Exmoor Pony Society will continue."

Everyone smiled and clapped as they turned round to look at Katy, who was doing a very good impression of a blushing goldfish.

CHAPTER 11
Wild and Free

Katy decided to let Trifle out onto the Common at the end of May — during half term — so Alice would be able to witness the great moment when Trifle was set free. The gestation period for horses and ponies is about 11 months. If Trifle did have a foal the following year, it would be born from the end of April onwards — the best time of year, because in the summer the weather is warmer and food is more plentiful.

Granfer and Alice came over to witness the historic moment, and the guests who were staying at Barton Farm for a painting weekend joined in, too. Katy was nervous, but confident that Trifle would take to her new-found freedom like a duck to water. After all, she had been born into the Barton herd, and had spent the first six months of her life on the Common.

Tom rode the quad bike out over the Common to find the ponies and bring them back to the gate. Katy waited, on the Common side of the gate, with Trifle and her crowd of well-wishers.

"It's so romantic!" said a lady from the painting course. "I think you're wonderful to set your pony free from the shackles of domesticity, Katy!"

At that moment, the herd came charging over the horizon; a thundering mass of hooves and bodies moving as one. Trifle's head shot up, her nostrils flared and she began to quiver with excitement.

"Let her go, Katy!" Granfer urged. "Quickly now, before the ponies get too near."

With shaking hands, Katy fumbled with the buckle on Trifle's head collar. Trifle was tossing her head and dancing around, which didn't make the task any easier. At last, the buckle was undone, and Trifle broke free. With her head held high and her tail raised like a flag, she galloped towards the ponies. The herd swerved, like a shoal of fish, and re-grouped behind Trifle, chasing her away over the Common and out of sight.

Katy felt totally empty. Everything had happened so quickly, and she had not even been able to say goodbye to Trifle properly.

"Ah! Bless them! Wasn't it lovely how they all went off to play together?" said the lady from the painting course.

Granfer looked worried. He knew the ponies weren't playing; they were chasing Trifle away because she was a stranger. It was a pity that Tom had excited them so much by herding them with the quad bike. Hopefully, they would calm down after a bit of a run around, and Trifle would be accepted into the herd. "Home for a cup of tea, I think," he said, trying to sound cheerful.

"Sounds good to me!" beamed the painting course lady.

They were all walking back across Moor Field when there was a dull thud of hooves behind them. They turned to see Trifle soaring over the Common gate, pursued by several Exmoor ponies who came to an abrupt halt when they reached the gate.

"Wow! I thought you said she couldn't jump!" Alice exclaimed.

Trifle galloped past at top speed and jumped another gate, heading for home as fast as her legs could carry her.

Katy found Trifle standing in her stable — luckily, the door had been left open. Trifle's sides were heaving and her body was covered in frothy white sweat. In the adjoining stable, Jacko munched on some hay and seemed totally unconcerned.

As Katy entered Trifle's stable, the pony gave her a look which said, "This is my home! Please let me stay here!"

It was clear that Katy would have two ponies to ride in the summer, and she would have to find a different stallion for Trifle. Her dreams of Trifle having a foal would not be realised for a while.

CHAPTER 12
Fire!

It was turning out to be a warm, dry summer. The tourists were very happy; they were getting a sun-drenched holiday without the hassle and expense of going abroad. The animals in the fields were not so happy; they melted into the shade of the beech hedges, trying to get away from the searing heat and an unrelenting plague of flies. Exmoor sizzled and shrivelled under the glare of the sun.

Babs was furious with Dean. He seemed to be spending all his time at Stonyford. Becoming obsessed with horses was something young girls did — not middle-aged men. It was ridiculous!

To be honest, Babs thought Dean was more interested in Melanie than the horses. Melanie was everything Babs was not: clever, stylish, natural, capable and confident. Babs felt isolated, useless and out of place on Exmoor. To combat her loneliness, she had a succession of friends to stay at Wellsworthy during the summer. They drove around the countryside, went to the beach and stayed up half the night — eating, drinking, smoking and making lots of noise. Dean felt as if his house had been invaded by parasites. He escaped to Stonyford as much as he could.

There was a record-breaking heat wave during the second week of August. One day, Babs and her guests decided that they would not join the queues of traffic heading for the beaches. Instead, they would go for a picnic on the Common. They loaded the Range Rover with a large disposable barbecue, disposable cutlery and plates, ready-made barbecue food, beer, cider and cigarettes. Then they drove over the Common, looking for a good picnic spot. Babs knew they were not supposed to drive over the Common in a car, but she could not understand why. As far as she could see, the moorland was just a useless, vast expanse of nothing, which made it an ideal off-road playground for people with four-wheel-drive vehicles. She did not care about the track of damaged heather and bare earth the Range Rover left in its wake.

Soon they found the ideal place: a pretty valley with a small stream running through it, surrounded by heather-clad slopes dotted with gorse bushes and hawthorn trees. The moorland was tinged with purple because the heather was just coming into flower. The air was heavy with scent. Insects hummed lazily between the plants.

The barbecue was not a great success. It took ages to light properly, so the food did not cook at all, and then it suddenly got extremely hot and burnt everything. They made up for the lack of food by drinking and smoking. When there was no more drink, they decided to go home.

"Give me the beach, any day," grumbled a man called Simeon as he shook insects off the picnic rug and put it in the Range Rover. Then he picked up the barbecue, and swore loudly. "It's still red hot! We can't put that in the car."

"Leave it there to cool down. We can come back later and pick it up," Babs said.

"Good idea," said Simeon. He lit a cigarette from the hot coals in the barbecue. "Oh, look! There's a paper plate in that gorse bush! The wind must have blown it there. Who'll volunteer to get it? I can't — I'm wearing sandals."

"Oh, just leave it!" Babs said irritably. "It's paper, so it'll rot away in time. Do you want to drive home, Simo, or shall I?"

"I will!" Simeon said eagerly.

The ground was rough and baked hard by the sun. Simeon found it rather difficult to keep control of the car while smoking a cigarette so, after he had driven a short distance, he threw the cigarette out of the car window.

The cigarette fell onto a patch of tinder-dry moor grass, which smouldered for several minutes and then burst into flames.

At the same time, the paper plate was dislodged from the gorse bush by a gust of wind. It floated through the air and came to rest on top of the barbecue. The plate developed a scorched brown patch which slowly spread out from the centre, and then it caught fire. The flames seemed to give the plate wings, and it landed on a clump of heather nearby. The heather caught alight instantly.

Within an hour, there were two fires on the Common. The first — caused by the discarded cigarette — moved slowly up the hill towards the highest ridge, fanned by a strengthening north-westerly breeze. The fire in the valley was much fiercer. Because the valley ran in a north-westerly direction towards the sea, the wind was perfectly placed to fan the flames upwards. The thick, dry heather ignited easily, and the gorse bushes crackled and popped with mini-explosions as they burned. When it reached the head of the valley, the fire was checked by boggy ground. The flames became less intense — producing thick, grey clouds of smoke as they crept in a south-easterly direction, gradually fanning out over the plateau at the top.

Earlier that day, the Barton herd of Exmoor ponies had moved to the highest ridge on the Common to make the most of the welcome breeze, which cooled them and helped keep the flies away.

Katy, Sharon and Alice were riding on the Common. Katy was on Trifle, Sharon was on Jacko and Alice was riding a lively young Arab mare called Sirocco, who had been sent to Stonyford for the summer in the hope that lots of work would calm her down. Trifle and Jacko walked steadily while Sirocco side-stepped, jogged and cantered on the spot. In between coping with her pony's antics, Alice was telling her friends all about Dean, who seemed to be spending a great deal of time at Stonyford. Dean seemed to be really nice; he wasn't the brash city slicker they had thought he was, but a kind, hardworking man with a great sense of humour. And he knew Robbie Williams — how cool was that? He was becoming a very good rider, too. Alice hoped that Dean and her mum would become more than just good friends.

As they came over the crest of the hill, they saw grey smoke rising up from the hills in front of them and mingling with the heat haze above.

"Holy smoke!" Katy exclaimed.

"Well, it doesn't look very holy to me, but it's definitely smoke," said Alice.

"Someone must have decided to do some swaling," said Katy.

"What's swaling?" Sharon asked.

"Burning the old heather and dead grass to make way for new growth and control the ticks and things," said Katy. "It's a traditional way of managing the moor. People are allowed to do it, if they get permission first."

"Not in the summer, though!" Alice corrected her. "You're not supposed to do any swaling from April until October. It harms ground-nesting birds and other wildlife, especially if it's dry — like it is now."

"Honestly, Alice! You're such a know-it-all sometimes!" Katy said, and regretted it instantly because Alice looked rather hurt. "I'm sorry, Alice! I meant that as a joke!"

"Well, that smoke doesn't look like a joke, anyway," said Sharon. "The fire looks pretty serious, to me."

"What shall we do?" asked Katy.

"We're nearer to Barton Farm than we are to Stonyford. Tom and Mark are baling silage in Moor Field, and I know Tom's got a mobile phone in his tractor, so let's go back to Barton and ring the fire brigade," Sharon said.

"Hang on a minute!" said Alice. "What are those black dots up on the ridge?"

"Oh, my goodness! They must be my ponies!" cried Katy. "There're going to get trapped by the fence at the top of the ridge if the fire keeps going. I've got to get them!"

"You can't go by yourself — I'll come, too," said Sharon.

" OK, then. I'll go back to Barton and get help," said Alice.

"Will you be all right by yourself?" Katy asked.

"I expect so. Sirocco behaves better when she's by herself," Alice said bravely.

Alice galloped off towards Barton Farm, and Katy and Sharon galloped towards the fire.

The irregular, fiery waves moving up the hillside made it look like an upside-down volcano. The flames consumed the colourful moorland, and left a blackened, smouldering wasteland on the lower slopes behind them. As Katy and Sharon got closer, they found that what they thought was one fire was, in fact, two. Although the wind was blowing the lines of flames towards each other, there was still an area which had escaped the fire in between. This, the girls decided, was the only route by which they could reach the Exmoor ponies and guide them to safety.

Trifle and Jacko were reluctant to go any closer to the fire, and the girls had great difficulty persuading them to enter the acrid smoke which hung over the hill. In places, the smoke made it hard to pick a sensible route through the heather and bracken. Several times, they had to re-trace their steps and change course. Fear gripped Katy. It felt like electric shocks running through her body and grabbing at her heart. Trifle was sweating, coughing and wheezing, but she kept plodding up the hill — steadfastly leading the way — to save the ponies who had chased her from the Common earlier in the year.

Eventually, they reached the top of the ridge, and relatively clean air. They stood for a minute, trying to get some fresh air into their lungs and work out what to do next. It was clear that their plan to drive the Exmoor ponies down the hill through the smoke was not going to work. The ponies were in a panic. The fire and the smoke had forced them onto the highest part of the Common, and they could go no further because of a boundary fence which ran along the top of the ridge. They were galloping to and fro along the fence line, looking for a way out. In their efforts to flee from the fire, some mares had become separated from their foals, which added to the confusion. The shrill whinnies of the foals were heart-rending.

All the time, the flames were travelling towards them like a marching army. There was only one way they could escape, and that was over the fence.

"We'll have to get the ponies to jump that fence, somehow," said Sharon.

"How can we do that? Drive them at it and hope they jump?"

"No, that would end in disaster. We'll have to break down the fence somewhere, and make it easier to jump. How about over there? It looks a bit more inviting over there," Sharon said.

"None of it looks inviting to me!" Katy said, as she followed Sharon to the fence. She could see what Sharon meant, though. If they had to jump the fence, that would be a good place to try. The ground was fairly even and on a gentle uphill slope.

The girls dismounted, and Katy held Trifle and Jacko while Sharon inspected the fence. Although the posts were old and the wire was rusty, the fence was going to be more difficult to break down than she had imagined. It consisted of sheep netting with two strands of barbed wire on top. The barbed wire was a problem. The girls were not wearing gloves or coats, so they had no means of protecting themselves from the sharp, vicious barbs which were placed at painfully short, regular intervals along the wire.

Trifle was itchy and covered with sweat. She pawed at the ground and then bent her front legs, preparing to roll.

"Trifle! Hup! Hup! Don't roll, you naughty girl! You'll ruin your saddle!" Katy cried in dismay.

"That's the answer! What a clever pony!" Sharon exclaimed. "We can put a saddle on top of the fence to protect us from the barbed wire, and lean on it to break the fence down!"

"That won't do the saddle much good," Katy said doubtfully.

"Well, do you have a better suggestion?"

"No."

"Come on, then! There's not a moment to lose!"

Trifle's saddle was the less valuable of the two, so Katy took it off her pony and placed it on top of the fence. With a deep sigh of satisfaction, Trifle got down and rolled. Katy did not stop her.

Sharon leant on the saddle and rocked it vigorously from side to side, trying to break the wire. The wire sagged a little, but did not break. Suddenly, with a splintering crack, a fence post broke off at ground level. The section of fence with the saddle on sank to half its original height.

"Hurray!" Katy shouted.

"Here, I'll hold the ponies. You see if you can get it down even more," Sharon said breathlessly. Her face was bright red and glistening with sweat.

Katy sat on the saddle and jumped up and down, as if she were doing rising trot. The wire buckled under her weight, but she could not get another fence post to break. All the time, the smoke was getting denser.

"That will have to do! The fire's getting too close!" Sharon shouted. "Quick! Put the saddle back on Trifle."

Katy wrestled with the girth on Trifle's saddle, while Sharon pulled up handfuls of grass and heather and piled them up against the broken-down fence, to cover the barbed wire and make the jump more visible. Trifle always blew her tummy out when her girth was done up, and now she was hot and sweaty, which made the task even more difficult. Finally, the saddle seemed to be secure, and Katy mounted. As soon as Katy put her weight in the stirrup, the saddle slid round and ended up under Trifle's tummy. Katy was filled with embarrassment and frustration.

Sharon was sitting on Jacko, ready for action. "Can you hop on and ride her bareback, Katy?" she asked.

Katy felt clumsy and useless. Vaulting was one of those things she had never been able to do, however much she tried. "Um, can you give me a leg-up?" she asked.

"No problem," said Sharon. She jumped off Jacko, gave Katy a leg-up onto Trifle, and then vaulted back onto Jacko — as if her limbs were made out of springs. "It's the Irish gypsy in me," she said modestly, seeing the admiration on Katy's face. "You go to the right and I'll go to the left, and we'll try to herd all the ponies back to this bit of fence."

The warm, sticky sweat from Trifle's back soaked into Katy's jeans. Trifle was not easy to ride bareback because she was like a barrel. Katy grabbed a handful of mane to steady herself, and urged her pony into a canter. They went in a sweeping arc around the ponies — like a dog rounding up sheep — and then pushed them gently along the line of the fence towards the broken section. The terrain was uneven and, despite the dry weather, boggy in places. Katy had to hang on tight as Trifle dodged tussocks and leapt boggy patches. Amazingly, Trifle seemed to know what the plan was, and Katy felt as if she were no more than a passenger.

The two groups of ponies were reunited — with much squealing and whinnying — and Katy and Sharon tried to drive the whole herd towards the jump they had made. To their dismay, the ponies were deeply suspicious of the unfamiliar obstacle, and refused to go anywhere near it. The sound of the fire was getting louder by the minute, and it was becoming hard to breathe the bitter, smoke-filled air. For the first time, they could feel the heat from the flames.

"I'll jump it first, to give the ponies a lead. You can push them on from behind. Try to keep them together. If it gets too dangerous, just get out," Sharon said, coughing between each word.

"I'll try," Katy said courageously.

Amazingly, everything went according to plan. With Jacko leading them and Trifle pushing them on, the Exmoor ponies leapt over the makeshift cross-country obstacle to fresh air and freedom, and galloped away over the adjoining moorland. At last, it was Katy's turn to ride Trifle over the jump, and not a minute to soon; the fire was creeping relentlessly towards the fence. Trifle flew at the jump and cleared it with ease.

Katy felt elated; it was the first time she had jumped Trifle bareback, and it had felt fantastic. Bareback — oh, dear! "My saddle!" Katy cried. She could see the saddle lying on the ground where she had left it. The flames were seconds away. Without thinking, Katy faced Trifle at the jump once more, and went back for the saddle. She slid off Trifle, picked up her saddle, threw it over the fence, vaulted onto Trifle and jumped back to safety.

Sharon hurried to pick up the saddle before the fire came through the fence. "For a pony who doesn't like jumping and a rider who can't vault, that wasn't bad!" she laughed.

"I did it, didn't I?" Katy gasped. "I actually vaulted!"

The rumble of engines could be heard above the noise of the fire, and a four-wheel-drive fire engine appeared over the moor behind them, followed by Mark in his tractor and Tom and Alice on a quad bike.

After making sure nobody was hurt, the firemen turned to getting the blaze under control.

Alice, Tom and Mark hurried over to Katy and Sharon.

"You took your time!" Katy said cheekily.

"Your fault for finding a fire that's so difficult to reach! We had to go right round by the top road. We'll go away again, if you're going to be so ungrateful," Tom said, smiling.

"Not so fast, mister!" Katy said. "We've got to go and find my Exmoor ponies!"

Soon after the fire, Babs left Exmoor forever. She went to live in Portugal, with Simeon.

CHAPTER 13
The Christening

Heather's christening took place in Simonsbath church on the first Sunday in December.

As Katy walked up to the door of the church, she saw Greg standing in the porch with Rachel and Mark. They were talking to the vicar. Greg looked even taller and more handsome than Katy had remembered, and his suntanned face contrasted with the pale, slightly blue complexions of the people around him. Katy's heart missed several beats, and she felt shy and awkward. She had to resist a strong urge to run away.

Greg saw Katy, and a broad smile lit up his face. "Hello, stranger!" he said. There was an Australian twang to his accent. "How are you doing, Katy?"

Katy felt completely tongue-tied.

Greg put his arm round Katy's shoulder and smiled down at her.

Katy was on cloud nine. She could not think of anything to say, so she just looked up at Greg, smiled shyly and said, "Hello."

Heather behaved remarkably well during the service. She didn't cry at all — not even when the vicar held her over the font, poured water over her forehead and baptised her. At eight months, she looked like the babies you see in advertisements for baby products; she was tubby, smiling and much more adorable than when she was newborn. Katy no longer felt ill at ease when she was asked to hold Heather or look after her for a little while — in fact, she enjoyed it.

After the christening, they all had lunch in the pub. Several friends of the family were invited, including Melanie, Dean and Alice, who had come back from boarding school for the weekend.

Melanie and Dean had a secret, but it wasn't a secret for long because of the gorgeous diamond engagement ring on Melanie's finger. Everyone was thrilled they were going to get married.

"Congratulations, mate," Greg said, shaking Dean's hand. "We've never met, but I feel I know you because I've heard a lot about you."

"Oh dear!" Dean smiled.

"No! All good, I assure you," Greg said. "I'm Greg, by the way — Mark's little brother."

"Good to meet you, Greg. Are you back on Exmoor for good, now?"

"Wish I were. If I could get a place to live and somewhere to farm, I'd come back like a shot. The trouble is that houses and land on Exmoor are so expensive now. Any house which does come up for sale becomes a second home or holiday let; it squeezes local boys like me out of the market. I'd love to live on Exmoor, but the truth is that there's much more opportunity to get on the farming ladder in Australia. I've been offered a share farming deal in Queensland, and I think I'm going to take it."

Katy overheard this. She walked away with a heavy heart, missing the rest of the conversation.

"I shouldn't be too hasty," Dean said. "How about coming over to Wellsworthy tomorrow evening? I've got an idea which may be of interest to you."

CHAPTER 14
Tinkerbell

"That Exmoor of yours is as big as a bus. What on earth are you feeding her?" Granfer said as he looked over the stable door.

"Only silage, Granfer. Honest!" Katy said, stroking Trifle's neck as she ate some food in a bucket. "Oh, and just a handful of nuts when she comes in at night. Jacko gets a good feed every night because he's fit and clipped out for all the competitions we're doing this winter. I don't want Trifle to feel left out, just because I'm not riding her very much at the moment."

"Well, you can easily kill ponies with kindness, you know," Granfer said. "If you give her too much food, she'll get laminitis, which will make feet so painful that she'll go hopping lame. Yes, laminitis is a terrible disease; some ponies never recover from it."

"I know, Granfer. We're taught about all that sort of thing at Pony Club. I must admit, she does seem to be getting pretty fat, doesn't she? But she's not at all lame. It's probably just her thick winter coat making her look big. I'll try to ride her a bit more, now it's the Christmas holidays."

"Good idea," Granfer said.

The following day, Katy discovered that Trifle really had become fatter. When she put the saddle on her pony, the girth was too short by a couple of inches. She decided to ride Trifle bareback, just down to Wellsworthy and back.

Trifle was unbelievably sluggish. Katy had to urge her pony on — even at walk. Katy was really worried. Perhaps Granfer was right; she had made Trifle ill from over-feeding her. Granfer's harsh words about killing ponies with kindness kept ringing in her ears. However, he had also said that exercise was a good idea. They were nearly at Wellsworthy, and Dean might be at home. He had become very knowledgeable about horses, and had read almost every equestrian book ever published. As Katy rounded the corner to Wellsworthy, she remembered the first time she had met Dean.

Katy's thoughts were interrupted by the sight of Greg's Land Rover parked in the lane. Greg was carrying a large box of belongings through the gate to Wellsworthy. He stopped and put the box down when he saw Katy.

"G'day, Katy! How are you doing?" Greg said.

"G'day, Greg. Good, thanks!" Katy answered, imitating his Australian accent.

"I just can't win!" Greg said, laughing. "In Australia, I was teased for having an English accent, and here I'm teased for talking like an Australian! Anyway, it looks as if you're the first person from Barton Farm to meet the new neighbour!"

"What do you mean?"

"Dean's living over at Stonyford now, but he doesn't want to sell Wellsworthy, so I'm renting it from him. I hope you don't mind."

"Mind! Why should I mind? I think it's really brilliant!" Katy exclaimed. Then, embarrassed by her own enthusiasm, she added, "You see, Dad and Tom were worried Wellsworthy might be converted into holiday lets, or sold again."

"Better the devil you know, eh?" Greg said, smiling.

"You could say that," Katy said, smiling back.

"Actually, I've got a job for you," Greg said. "Will you design a label for me?"

"What sort of label?" Katy asked, mystified.

"A mineral water bottle label. An Exmoor scene with Wellsworthy Water above it would be good."

"Surely, nobody round here is going to buy water in bottles! There's water everywhere you look on Exmoor, and it's free! What on earth gave you such a crazy idea?" Katy exclaimed.

"You did."

"Me?"

"Yes. You sent me that bottle of water in Australia. It made me realise how much we take water for granted on Exmoor, and what a valuable commodity it is when it's scarce, as it is in Australia. I started to think that, if I were ever lucky enough to get somewhere to live on Exmoor, I would set up a business bottling water. When Dean offered me Wellsworthy, it was too good to be true. Wellsworthy has always been famous for its plentiful supply of natural spring water — hence the name."

"Is Dean OK about it all?"

"He thinks it's a great idea. The farm has only 65 acres with it, so I'll have to do something besides farming to make ends meet. Selling water seems to be the answer. Despite what you think, there's a growing market for mineral water, even in England. In fact — believe it or not — it's often more expensive to buy than milk. But, unlike milk, it has a very long shelf life. So, have I managed to persuade you I'm not off my rocker?

Katy giggled. "Just about."

"And will you design that label for me, please?"

"Of course I will."

"Proper job. I'll drop in to see your family later, if that's OK."

"We'll look forward to it. I'll tell Dad to get the whisky bottle out," Katy said. Phil was famous for the generous measures of whisky he gave to visitors.

"At least I'll be able to walk home from Barton, now I'm living here!" Greg said.

Trifle seemed to have gone to sleep on her feet while Greg and Katy were talking.

Katy roused her pony. "See you later!" she

said to Greg. Then, she and Trifle walked sedately round the corner and headed home. Trifle seemed to be a bit more eager on the way home, and Katy's earlier concerns about her pony were put to one side because of her excitement about Greg moving into Wellsworthy. She couldn't wait to tell her family the good news.

Needless to say, everyone at Barton Farm was delighted to hear the news about Greg. As promised, he went to the farm that evening. As anticipated, he walked home.

Katy hardly slept at all that night; she was worried about Trifle again. When she had looked at the ponies before bedtime, Trifle had looked uncomfortable and restless. Perhaps she was getting colic. At five o'clock in the morning, Katy's anxieties got the better of her, and she decided to go out and check her pony.

Outside, it was cold, dark and raining. Katy shivered as she walked to the stable — she felt tired and her stomach was churning. In the old cow shed, which had been converted into stables for her two ponies, she switched on the light. Jacko had been sleeping standing up. He woke with a start.

Trifle was already wide awake. She appeared to be eating the straw in the corner of her box, which was odd because there was still plenty of silage left in her hay rack. Katy peered into the dimly-lit stable. Trifle lifted her head, and Katy's heart leapt. Her mind could not believe what her eyes were telling her. There, nestled in the far corner of the stable, was a perfect, wonderful, adorable, magical, tiny foal!

Very carefully, Katy entered Trifle's stable and went over to the foal. At the same time, she kept an eye on the mare to make sure she did not mind. If anything, Trifle seemed to be glad that Katy was there. The foal was very new; it was still damp, and steam rose from it into the cold early morning air. Katy rubbed the little creature with straw to dry it and get its circulation going. Then, she helped it to its feet to drink some life-giving first milk, known as colostrum, from its mother. All the while, Katy talked in a soothing voice: "There's a good girl. What a clever pony you are, Trifle. What a clever girl. There we are. Shall we try a drink, then? Clever old girl...."

The foal suckled greedily from its mother, and then sank back onto the straw again. Katy sat down beside the foal, with her back against the stable wall, and stroked it as it slept. It was unusually hairy for a newborn foal. Nature seemed to have given it a fluffy winter coat. Nature was pretty wonderful. In fact, everything was pretty wonderful, Katy thought, as she drifted off to sleep.

An hour later, Tom found Katy asleep in Trifle's stable, her arms draped over a dozing newborn foal. Trifle was lying down close by. Where on earth had the foal come from? Had Katy found it on the moor? There was no way it could be Trifle's. Oh, help! Yes there was! The night the ponies raided the silage, of course! Now Tom's secret would come out!

News of the foal spread rapidly amongst Katy's friends and relations. Soon Alice, Melanie, Dean, Granfer, Greg, Sharon and Rachel were all crowded into Trifle's stable as the good-natured pony munched on some silage.

"What are you going to call it? Is it a he or a she?" Alice asked.

"I've been so excited, I haven't even looked!" Katy said. She examined the foal quickly. "It's a she!" she announced.

"So, what are you going to call her, then?" Alice asked.

"I've absolutely no idea."

"That's rather a long name!" Alice teased.

"And the championship goes to Katy Squires on I've Absolutely No Idea!" she said, pretending to talk through a loudspeaker.

Everyone laughed.

Alice and Katy spent the rest of the morning, and most of the afternoon, thinking about possible names for the foal while they decorated the Christmas tree at Barton Farm.

"How about Christmas Pudding, or Holly?" suggested Alice. "It should be something to do with Christmas."

"Mm, but I want to carry on the Barton herd tradition of the foal's name starting with the first letter of the dam's name. So the name has got to start with T," said Katy.

"Tinsel!" Alice said triumphantly, arranging some tinsel around the tree.

"Perhaps," Katy said doubtfully. "I'd like it to tie in with the stallion's name, too."

"You don't want much, do you?" Alice joked. She tried to remember the characters in the story of Peter Pan. "Nana? Wendy?" she said hesitantly. "Hey! Wasn't it funny when Tom told everyone about the ponies raiding the silage? I don't know how he managed to keep that a secret!"

Katy giggled. "As Granfer said, the truth always comes out in the end," she said. "Poor old

Trifle! If only I'd known she was pregnant, I'd never have ridden her all summer — especially not into the fire to rescue the ponies. And I even rode her yesterday! I must have been blind not to notice she was in foal!"

"You weren't to know. Anyway, the foal's fine — a proper little tinker. Oh, look! Here's the fairy for the top of the tree."

"That's it! You're a genius, Alice!"

"What?"

"The foal's name, of course! Something to do with Christmas and the story of Peter Pan, and beginning with T! Tinkerbell! She was the fairy in Peter Pan, wasn't she?"

"Eureka! We've done it!"

"Hurray for Tinkerbell! Wheee! Whoops! Oh! Hello, Greg!"

Greg was standing in the doorway, looking highly amused. "Have you ladies been at the Christmas sherry? Sally asked me to tell you that tea's ready."

Christmas Eve tea at Barton Farm had become a traditional feast. All the family were there: Phil, Sally, Katy, Tom, Granfer, Gran, Rachel, Mark and Heather. Several friends had also been invited: Melanie, Dean, Alice, the twins, Sharon and Greg.

They ate, drank, talked and played games until the evening turned into the night.

"Dad always says that the farm animals talk at midnight on Christmas Eve, don't you, Dad?" Phil commented, as he dealt some cards.

"And do they?" Dean asked. He was beginning to realise that anything was possible on Exmoor.

"Well, not in a language I can understand, anyway!" Granfer chortled.

It was nearly midnight when the guests left. Katy put on her coat and boots, and went outside to check Trifle, Tinkerbell and Jacko. They were all fine.

"Goodnight, Trifle. My wonderful, clever pony!" Katy said. "Goodnight, Tinkerbell. Goodnight, Jacko. Happy Christmas."

As Katy left the stable, she was sure she heard Trifle say, "Night, night!"

What a lot can happen in one year, Katy thought, when she woke up on Christmas morning. Sharon had become a good friend, Jacko was fit and well again, Heather had been born, Trifle had overcome her fear of jumping, Granfer had given Katy the Exmoor ponies, they had escaped that terrible fire, Melanie and Dean were going to get married, Greg was living at Wellsworthy and

Trifle had given birth to Tinkerbell. Things just couldn't get any better than that, could they?

Katy sighed with happiness and stretched out in her warm bed. Her feet bumped against something. It was a bulging Christmas stocking, waiting to be explored.